T0191116

Ruined a Little When We Are Born

"In these stories, whole lives, marriages, births, deaths, and afterlifes unfold in the words and blank spaces of just a few pages. The stories build on one another—sensory, sensual, pulsing with life and color—leaving the reader breathless and starstruck by the wildly inventive twists of Zambrano's vibrant prose."

—Alex DiFrancesco, author of *Transmutation*

"In her captivating new collection, Zambrano deftly blurs the lines between reality and fantasy, weaving together narratives that explore the surreal within the confines of the everyday. Each story is a masterclass in brevity and depth, in precision and elegance. A stunning and remarkably original collection."

—Andrew Porter, author of *The Disappeared*

"The short stories in Zambrano's new collection, *Ruined a Little When We Are Born,* crackle with life, energy, mystery, and passion. Here you will find twists of fate, heartaches, dreams, children, animals, mothers and fathers, gods and goddesses. Lovers leave. The dead come back. Dawn bursts into the room. Told in precise, razor-sharp sentences, these are stories that cut cleanly and deep."

—Steve Edwards, author of *Breaking into the Backcountry*

"Fast-paced plots, razor-sharp writing, and so apt imagery! Short, snappy, surprising, sensual, and sometimes even shocking, *Ruined a Little When We Are Born* is a unique and playful collection in which each story tells us a lot more in just a few pages and leaves us with an invigorating experience."

—Aruni Kashyap, Director of Creative Writing,
University of Georgia

RUINED A LITTLE
WHEN WE
ARE BORN

— STORIES —

TARA ISABEL ZAMBRANO

DZANC
BOOKS

DZANC BOOKS

2580 Craig Rd.
Ann Arbor, MI 48103
www.dzancbooks.org

Library of Congress Cataloging-in-Publication Data Available Upon
Request

ISBN: 9780983740582
First US edition: October 2024
Interior design by Michelle Dotter
Cover design by Sarah Shields

Printed in the United States of America

10   9   8   7   6   5   4   3   2   1

CONTENTS

To my mother with love

MOTHER, FALSE

THE GIRL GROWS OVERNIGHT after her mother dies—two extra hands emerge from her back, like the Hindu goddess Durga. Her forehead is lashed with lines. Her mother's curses roll on the surface of her tongue. They fall and clog the drains. The girl's extra hands work as a plunger, extend to the fridge to pick items, fan air on humid days. She starts wearing her mother's clothes—oversized skirts and blouses and a stained apron, her eyes deliberately keen like a hawk's. From the park bench, she watches her siblings: the six-year-old and the toddler on the swing, up and down the slides, the teenager on the monkey bars, his scrawny arm barely strong enough to hold on, his fingers slipping. They laugh and run. There's love in their voices, but not enough to call her Ma.

Before her mother died, the girl considered herself an atheist, but now she lights an incense and an earthen lamp every evening, bows her head in front of the metal idols of Krishna and Vishnu lit in orange glow. She whispers *OM* a hundred and eight times like her mother used to. She wipes the dust off her mother's framed photo taken at her wedding—her chin lowered, her eyes gazing into her hennaed palms lifted close to her face, the light coming at a slant on her cheeks and forehead, reflecting from the edges of her fingers. She looks radiant, unlike how the girl remembers her when she died.

But the girl decides this is how she'll think of her mother, beautiful, confident like she knows her mind.

Most nights, her father falls asleep on the couch, an empty bag of potato chips crunching under his frame. Double-chinned and balding. TV on, volume down. Documentaries on wars and planes. Natural disasters. Sometimes he pours a double scotch, sips, and watches the twisted branches of the banyan on the patio, the hinged wings of the warbler, a slow grief accumulating on his face. Then he takes out his handkerchief and wipes his brow. The front door is always unlatched because he goes out and comes in at odd times. The girl starts calling him by his name.

Days splinter. Her hands smell of garlic and garam masala, fingers curved inward because of constantly holding things. Sometimes, the girl feels she was born a mother. The feeling is so old that only her young reflection in the mirror reminds her she is still a girl. Her transformation strange as the fact that they haven't been out of monsoon, but the wind only brings in the dust and debris through the cracks of the windows and the space below the doors. The sky is crowded with clouds like an unmade bed and rain has left them as all breathing things do. To conserve resources, the girl showers once a week, the water muddy as it drapes around her. The toddler sleeps curved like a bean, his nose pressed into her neck, trying to sniff the semblance between their mother and her. When the teenager plays the violin, suddenly off-key, she reminds him to keep the music simple, carve out the sour notes and start again. At night, her extra hands shuffle through the dark, reach the faces of her siblings and run fingers through their hair, feel the rush of their breath blowing north, press their foreheads with blessings. The girl has varicose veins because of standing too long in the kitchen preparing dal and rotis, scrubbing the greased pressure cooker and the karahi. She chases the kids in her dreams.

Sometimes the girl's mother appears in the doorway between the kitchen and the patio. "No help will come for you, you'll only grow hands, one pair from another, light-year after light-year, and still, it will never be enough," she says in her usual high-pitched singsong voice, continues with her tense sips of air as if she's still breathing. The girl massages her mother's scalp—there are dead insects, dried leaves, dirt—as if it's a little ritual to make her feel at home. Her extra hands swat the flies. Steam from a pot of boiling rice curls in their hair like cobwebs. She offers a bowl of stir-fried veggies, boiled eggs. Her mother's mouth opens like a dark, wide hole where all her children can fit. She swallows the food without chewing. "In afterlife, there's no metabolism, only hunger," she says. From the drawn curtains, the sun pokes their eyes. The girl touches her mother's blue-cooled skin, love handles around her waist, the rice-bowl cavity of her chest and senses a pulse—not enough to be a heartbeat, only a memory of a life that once was.

"I'll never be whole to reincarnate as long as all my kids are living," complains her mother, her fingers fluttering like wings. For a moment, everything is quiet, then a hush of her mother's sigh like a day turning over a page.

Her father walks into the kitchen. "You are talking to yourself," he says. Her mother half-smiles listening to the sound of her husband's deep-throated voice, the slight dark between his lips that separates memory from loss. She watches him walk into his room and close the door behind him. Then she plucks the girl's extra, worn-out hands like two bad teeth.

"What will I do after the children grow up and leave?" the girl asks her mother.

"You will raise your shortcomings as your own child, one that will always stay."

The girl looks at her mother's glinted eyes. She has so many questions but is unable to find the right words.

"Women have a hard time in this world, but I have high hopes for you," she says, and pinches the girl's cheeks for good measure before she disappears. The girl feels all the tears inside her rocket like bubbles in a soda bottle. She lets herself weep, needful and gasping. Until she is left with hiccups. Until her face is glazed milky in the moonlight. She wipes the snot with the tail of her apron and unties it. The holes her extra pair of hands have left feel hollow like a contracted womb of a hand-me-down mother-who-never-birthed-a-child, who craves her own mother. She wraps her discarded hands in an old towel and places them under her bed. At night, she hears them scratch the floor, crawling back and forth as if unsure what to look for. How to search another source of blood, another body, another mother to mobilize them.

THE GIRL WITH A PAINTED TONGUE

A GIRL IN MY class paints her tongue with a different color every day. When I see her, she sticks out her tongue—blue, yellow, lavender. "It's rude to do that," I say, and she does it again. In class, she sits on the last bench, and I can feel her eyes on my back. When I turn around, she's not there. The teacher takes roll call, and someone says, "Yes," when her name is called.

The girl has unusually long legs and arms. Her palms are also painted. Smooth, no life line, no marks. She carries a mirror with her, uses it to focus light and burn bugs. When she laughs language falls out on the ground like pebbles shaking with sound.

In my dreams, the girl plucks my eyelashes and makes a string. She inserts the string in my mouth. "I am pulling out your soul," she says.

"Why?" I ask, coughing, about to throw up.

"Because I don't have one," she says. I wake up out of breath, my hand over my chest, my heart so loud I get a headache. When I tell my classmates about the dream, they push me and laugh, call me crazy. Watching from a corner, the girl sticks the tip of her tongue out.

I instruct the girl to stop appearing in my dreams.

"I have no control," she claims, and moves the mirror in her hand, flickering light around me, making me dizzy. "I cannot stop," she says in her singsong voice. "Cannot. Stop."

"Go away," I yell. She shakes her head and pushes the mirror in the pocket of her overalls. "What do you want?" I ask.

"I want to play with you," she says. Her tongue is oxblood red like Indian goddess Kali. She pulls out a doll from her pocket. Blonde hair, brown eyes, black wool dress.

"This doll can talk," she says and hands it to me.

"Is that so?" The doll looks at me, sticks out her tongue. I almost drop it.

"You can have her," the girl says.

"No, it's fine," I say, and throw the doll on the floor. The doll gets up and floats in the air, raises her hands. Her palms are painted.

"Shit!" I scream, and run to my class. The girl and the doll follow me, disappear when I run inside the room. Everyone is looking at me, whispering. The girls who pushed me are looking at each other, pointing their fingers at me, giggling. The teacher makes me stand in the corner for being late. She asks me why my palms are painted.

After school, when the bus comes, the girl with the painted tongue is back. She sits behind me, quiet. Then she passes me a bag of tortilla chips, orange, flaming hot, my favorite. I look away as if I don't know her and continue licking my palms to get rid of the color, a metallic taste setting in my mouth.

"I am having a party," she whispers in my ear, "You should come. You're the only friend I got." I think of all the times when I wanted someone to invite me to their birthday and let me play with their toys and sit cross-legged on their bed, comfortable to share secrets. Tears stream down my face. I turn around and look at her.

"Where's your doll?"

"I threw it away because she bothered you," the girl says. Her eyes, soft and wet.

We are rounding up a mountain. The bus is close to the edge, almost flying. This isn't the way to my home, but it's beautiful wherever we are going. The valley below is filled with trees with painted leaves, little tongues hanging out, little palms with life lines etched on them. She pulls out the mirror and turns it toward me. I stick my tongue out. In my reflection, she does the same.

FEVER

THE DAY IS RUNNING a fever of 46 degrees Celsius when I fall for Sharad. Strong, tall, he strides confidently toward the office where we both work. My body breaks a sweat as I raise my eyes to catch all of him in a single gaze.

·

The first time I wake up in his bed, I shake slightly at his slow-heart breathing. The black turf of his hair on the long pillow we share. His eyes are shut when he says my name—the syllables drown on the slippery edge between dreams and wakefulness. I walk out of the sheets and morning light acquires me. A blackbird with its distinct beak and bright eye-ring stares at me from the leafy green confetti of a mango tree.

·

In the conference room, I run a fever, and so does Sharad—we have caught a bug from eating pani puri in New Market, the kind with extra spicy mint chutney and tamarind sauce. In the evening, when the sun rubs stardust on the clouds, we lie shivering, kissing, the ibuprofen cooling us. Then we doze off, our backs pressed against each other like a planet touching its own reflection.

•

On a wet Basant Panchami day in February, we marry. Our wedding is a simple affair, family and a few close friends. The henna illustrates my hand in a paisley pattern, *Sharad* written in a column of roses on my right-hand index finger. He's wearing sherwani-churidar and I am wearing a mauve lehenga. That night, in a suite at Le Méridien, tired of the ceremonies, we fall asleep on a bed decorated with jasmine garlands, barely touching each other.

•

Our apartment faces east-west. The sun bends our indoor plants in its direction, an enchanter. We paint the walls blush pink, saffron, oxblood red. For my nightdress I wear Sharad's white cotton kurta, scented with his aftershave, sweat, and talcum powder. I don't wash it because it's passing through time, warm with familiarity, soft at its seams.

•

The fever is a constant companion when I root his semen into me and grow a baby. "To give breath to another is the most sacred thing we can do as humans," my mother says, her hands massaging my swollen feet, my warmer skin recoiling at her soft, cool touch, afraid to lose its fervor. The monsoon has begun, and the damp earth makes me nauseous. A layer of sweat sits on me. I cannot tolerate Sharad's touch.

•

As the day of delivery nears, I grow hotter in body and colder in attitude. Sharad cooks, and I throw up. I drop things and stand amidst scattered glass like a nervous child. He reaches the dark spaces under the dishwasher, under the cabinets with the long neck of the vacuum, the back of his head exposed with thinning hair.

·

Nights, I hardly sleep. I watch the dark condensing as dew in our yard from the bedroom window. The moon rises aimlessly—a balloon— and I wonder if somewhere west the sun is still golden over a boy and girl like Sharad and me, awkwardly kissing for the first time in the back seat of his parents' car. I'll never know those people, I think.

·

Sharad's mother comes to help with the newborn. The baby has wrinkled skin and cupid lips. A butt-chin. In a rectangle of warmth from the skylight, Sharad's mother places the baby on his back and rubs olive oil on his tiny torso, his frail legs. "This will give you strength to catch up with the world," she says as she folds his legs to his chest and straightens them. After the massage, she lowers the baby into my lap and he falls asleep, a ribbon of drool running from his mouth to his chin. I touch his slick, rounded body—soft elbows, knees, little nose. "Some days we'll crawl under the bed, and you'll tell me about Treasure Island," I whisper, my lips close to his forehead, a film of his tender breath intermingled with mine.

·

The clock empties hours into the walls. Shadows lengthen and shorten, but I feel less and less like me. The calendar on the wall is marked with our baby's growth. After feeding him, I feel like an empty bowl. Every shirt of mine smells of drool and milk, outlines of spills visible on the fabric despite several stain removers and wash cycles. My ears have tuned in to the baby's sleeping breath, his waking yawn, even the blinking of his eyes. It's tiring to hear so much.

·

Nights are harder even with their silence. Maybe it's a flaw in me—I should learn to cultivate the mother in me, instead of wondering: where does one go to be alone?

•

Some nights, I walk to my son's crib and watch him shudder in his sleep, then smile, twisting his face into shapes I don't understand. I call my mother and ask her about it.

"He is shaking off his past lives, his old good and bad karma," says my mother.

I start crying.

"What's wrong?" she asks.

"I stand by his crib and am unable to move. Unable to do anything else, think anything else," I say.

"It will pass," she says, and I feel a sudden tenderness for my mother, for enduring all my growing years. After disconnecting the phone, I watch two clouds in the sky, drifting, almost overlapping each other, and then apart, framing the sun in the center.

I want to hold Sharad, but weighted with work, his back leans against a chair. He's no longer the pillar I once had. His hands are full of grocery bags and diapers. His chest, my safe place to cry, come, and fist my anger is now lit by the glare of his work computer screen—Amazon Prime is always open in the corner. Our house is full of objects, and I feel I have lost him.

We start before daybreak to drive to Udaipur for a wedding. On our way, I watch the transmission lines, cell towers slicing the light, the baby asleep in his car seat. Sharad has lost weight and I have gained some and yet we have packed the dresses and suits we wore at our own wedding. They are buried, crumpled under formula and jars of baby food. When he hits the brakes, I can hear the clank of baby spoons against the sippy cups, the plastic rattle of a box of wipes.

"Are you with me?" he asks.

"Yes," I say, and turn to look at him.

"Now you are," he says and smiles. The thrilled mischief in his eyes, his dimpled cheeks, the braid of muscles sloping from his neck into his collarbones. Outside the sun is inching, and the surfaces of lakes and pastures are covered with the feverish pink of the morning.

"We're doing good time," I say.

"Yes, how far we have come," he says, a softness in his voice. I can't make sense of how it feels. Something sad and happy, a deep-blue feeling like this space between us even when our hands are touching while passing the baby, when our feet are brushing in our sleep—this air of equilibrium with a lukewarm temperature of marriage. Like going down and up on an escalator but never landing.

·

In the opposite lane, I see a convoy of standing vehicles. The hood of a car is smashed underneath the side of a truck, perfectly interlocked as if never to separate. The drivers in our lane have slowed down and then picked up their speed, moving on, feeling grateful it's not them. I keep looking at the crash from the side-view mirror and realize both of us will turn thirty-five this fall. Inside I know there are things I want to do, but they retreat further and further away like the collision in the rearview mirror.

"Do you think we'll love each other forever?" I ask and regret it right away because it sounds stupid. Sharad chuckles and starts humming a song, his voice oddly young, as if it came from a time before I knew him. Before we cracked open our hearts for each other without knowing if they'd be whole again.

I understand now that what I fear most is us lasting longer than I can love.

I join his singing. He rolls down the window. And somewhere in the lyrics, he answers my question. Ahead, the highway flattens into a straightaway with no trees in sight. A pair of dull-looking gray birds from the roadside take flight and dive into the tender sky.

GHOSTS OF THE UNBORN

THE SNAKES ARE DEAD. In the backyard, my husband is piling them on top of each other, their skin crimping in the summer heat. When he comes inside, he's covered in sweat, snake bites on his feet. Outside the cicadas are screeching at full power. I want to call a clinic, but he says he is feeling fine.

"How do you know?" I ask him.

He slaps his hand on the kitchen counter. "I just do."

He comes out of the shower and his eyes are glazed over.

"We should burn the dead snakes because according to a Hindu tradition, it releases the spirit once the body turns to ash and the snakes at least deserve that," I say. He nods his head in agreement. We pick up the fleshy, slippery pile, drop it into an old clay urn, and set it on fire, smoke swirling from our yard. Later, lying on our bed, he nibbles my ear, his hand rough on my breast.

"Why did you kill them? We used to enjoy watching them slithering on the grass, looping across each other like loose knots."

"They were multiplying like crazy. Every time I stepped in the yard, they'd hiss and wake up under my feet, over them."

I stare at the bite marks.

He waves his hand in dismissal. From the bedroom window, I see the daffodils and tulips, a nest up in the Bradford pear, a round bush from which a piece of polyester twine is unraveling. As the golden hour ticks its last, the sky is specked with clouds, silver scaled at the horizon.

The next time my husband kisses me, his tongue's edge is a soft divider sweeping my cheeks. He clicks it in his sleep. Then he gets up and wanders in the yard. At dawn, he taps our bedroom window, puts his palm on the glass, baby scales twitching on his skin. He says he wants to slither inside my body as if it were a dark, wet hole. He licks the window and hisses, a wet curve on the glass. The birds at the feeder shriek, they swirl over his head before flying away. I call him inside and his boots ring out sharply on the tiles.

His eyes are still, stoned while he moves above me, and in be-tween, he slips down so expertly I wonder. His tongue fully forked between my legs. I twinge with pleasure. He softly bites into my pinkie as he used to before and raises his head as if he remembered something. He scurries away, brings a knife to the bed, and chops off my digit. I scream so loudly he's unable to move.

"Why?" I say when I can breathe.

"Because you might die of my poison spreading in your blood."

I stare at the finger turning blue, then purple, curling like a dried-up worm. He picks it up like a baby, walks away. I look outside the window. He is digging a hole in the yard.

"I want you to be as before," I say, when he comes in to clean up.

"That's not happening." A low grunt in his voice, his bare back slimmer as if his ribs have shrunk, his hips caved in. I touch his waist. It's mushy as if there are no bones, just cartilage and muscle.

"Stop that," he wheezes. I quietly cry for a few minutes and watch him breathe, his body blanketed in a cloud of steam. His jaw opens and shuts, bubbles surfacing and flattening. He tries to circle inside but hits the porcelain.

"I love you," I say. His face, half-submerged, begins to show some other expression than anger, maybe sorrow, maybe loss, and I cannot get that image out of my head. What he's experiencing, I realize, I am not, even though in some ways our lives are still overlapped. An hour later, he's back in the yard digging and digging until he manages to slide in. The trees are alive with tiny, impatient birds.

In the morning I open the back door and he is coiled outside the hole. He crawls to the patio, his hood raised, his breath strong, furious. I let him hang on my forearm, bring him in, place him in a shallow filled tub. Later in the day, he stays on the grass, his head turned toward the place where we burned the snakes. Charred flakes in the urn. He slithers into it and zigzags out covered in ash.

The next time I see him, he has a dead rat in his mouth. There is another snake with him, slender, probably female. He wraps his tail around her. I hold my breath. They slither in the yard. Alert, lusty, or so I imagine. I close my eyes and think of his hand curling around my leg. When I open my eyes, they are gone. I wait the entire day for him to surface. Something is lost between us, and I feel I'll never find it again. The utensil in the corner sits empty, darkening in the fading light.

It rains for the next few days. The yard is puddled. When the air is steeped with sun, I step outside and there are four oblong eggs snuck in cool shade between the fence and the bald cypress. Spiky green leaves have started shooting out of the side of the tree's branches. Pearls of rain lodged in the flowers. Before I know it, I am hitting them with the same stick my husband used to kill the snakes, their sap glazing the grass, their shells like teeth, sharp edges up. Then I run inside and cry in the shower, the skin around my absent pinkie growing, gauzing the wound in absence.

Thereafter, day after day, I lie in bed, noosed in loneliness, waiting to hear a rustle in the yard. New birds come to the feeder and go. One of them a startling yellow and black. Butterflies stagger, orange wings smudged at the edges as if with mascara. Leafy weeds have grown up where I found the eggs, their leaves fanned out facing the window, fine spider silk running between them as if representing the ghosts of the unborn. The sun paints the horizon red and then pink before the legs of the sky close for the night. Every time the breeze hits the leaves, I turn my head toward the direction where his hole is and wonder if I could slide in what would I find—damp dirt, debris, a shimmering darkness, or a long, dark body, ready to claw, raised like a hook.

SHABNAM SALAMAT

SOMEONE FILLED ABBA'S HOOKAH during the daawat of his recent wedding. When he inhaled, it sounded like the hiss of the wind in the valley, the sound that kept Ammi, my mother, awake at nights, and her guilt of not being able to give him a son. The house smelled dense with fresh mutton, Abba's favorite but oldest goat, Mustafa's head lying in the corner of the verandah, eyes wide, pleading.

I was serving rose sherbet to the women seated in a single row of plastic chairs when Abba's new bride, Shabnam, twenty-two—a year older than me—yawned and raised her arms, her skin glossy like a plastic doll, a slim line of her hair running from her navel to her salwar. The men surrounding Abba glanced at Shabnam's flat waist, the tight bud of her navel. Horrified, Ammi ran to her, "Ya Allah, besharam."

"Nafisa." Abba cleared his throat and raised his hand. Ammi halted. Standing at the doorstep that led to the kitchen, I held the empty tray close to my chest like it was a flotation device. In the background, the folk song sounded like weeping, an older woman prayer-drifted through the rosary, blessing the new couple, "Shabnam Salamat, Rafiq Salamat."

•

On my bed, Ammi cried for hours as if she borrowed the rain. In the living room, on a diwan, spread-eagled in his floral patterned sherwani, Abba watched TV, his dark-circled, rheumed eyes opened and closed like a carnivorous flower.

Shabnam dragged her red suitcase toward Abba and Ammi's bedroom.

"Chudail, " Ammi spat, lined curses between the kitchen and the bedroom that drowned in the sound of the news. I glanced at Abba's bedroom, a pale yellow light, a new red-and-white checkered sheet on the bed against the wall from where the plaster had been falling these past few months, an old green vase on the side table with three legs, a metal rod substituting as the fourth.

Shabnam stood in the doorway of the bedroom as if she was unsure whether to step inside. Ammi was in the kitchen now, her knife furiously hitting the concrete platform, chopping onions for the keema as she sniffled and cursed her watery eyes. I walked toward Shabnam and placed a hand on her shoulder.

Inside the bedroom, I unlocked the steel almirah that always made a sound like the ground was quaking and groaning. I pointed to the shelf Ammi had cleared for Shabnam's clothes.

"Is this always locked?" Shabnam pointed to the almirah.

"Yes, Ammi sleeps with this under her pillow though there isn't anything valuable here." I dangled the solitary key hanging from a wire that went through a faded handkerchief, like a pendulum. Shabnam grinned. A mole on her chin, the sound of her laughter soft.

"Why don't you arrange your things except what you need for the night?"

"There isn't enough room to put in all my stuff," Shabnam whispered, then stared directly at me. Flustered at my inability to help, I shrugged.

"I feel so hot," she said and threw her golden-red dupatta on the bed. "Where's the bathroom?" she asked, stretching her hands in the air, the underarms of her ruby kurta sweat-darkened in the shape of a map of Kashmir. I helped her put the suitcase on the bed. She opened it and pulled out a bath towel.

Ammi's footsteps approached us.

"You shouldn't take a bath now," I whispered.

Shabnam glanced at the bedroom door.

"Cold water bath after sunset will result in sneezing and a runny nose, eventually a sore throat." Ammi said, her voice laced with authority.

Once again, I felt bad for Shabnam. The way I felt when the imam was reading the terms and conditions of her Nikah. The way she kept pressing her palms together, turning her head toward Abba, trying to get a glimpse of him. Thinking of my father with her, I felt a hot knot under my tongue, the back of my throat hitching. My stomach turned.

Shabnam sighed and sat on the bed. The summer heat perceptible in snaking tendrils of hair clinging to her cheeks and forehead. Her eyes caught in confusion and the blur of an unwelcoming household. I wondered in that moment if this was ever the wedding day Shabnam imagined since she was a little girl. Without the disco, ear-throbbing music that our generation loved, without laughter. Her absent family. Seeing her work here was done, Ammi asked me to accompany her to a nearby store.

I stepped outside the bedroom, leaving Shabnam with her suitcase and her thoughts. In the corner of the living room sat Abba's comfort ebony chair which was probably as old as his marriage to Ammi. On the beige wall, a six-by-ten framed photograph of Ammi posing on the edge of this chair, in her soft pink bridal wear, the henna of her palms visible, her golden bangles two sizes larger than her wrists. In the chair was my father, twelve years her senior, his hair slick and pulled back, debonair in his three-piece suit and white leather shoes. They looked happy and in love. Until the following seven years of prayers and visits to dargah and shrines of spiritual men gave them a daughter and not a son. At that time, Abba was a manager in a sugar mill, until ten years later, when there was a strike and the mill closed indefinitely. He was already past forty-five and didn't want to leave his ancestral home. He found some jobs along the way and sold some of my grandfather's real estate and Ammi's jewelry to get by.

Outside, geckos and squirrels rushed in the waning light.

"Why would Shabnam agree to marry an older man like Abba?" I asked Ammi on the way.

"Shabnam has been living with her grandparents, taking care of them. Her two much older sisters are married and settled in Dubai. And she would have had the same fate. But in the last three months there had been trouble."

"A stalker?" I asked.

"Yes." Ammi lowered her voice. "Rumor rose that he was a militant from the other side of the valley. Obviously, Shabnam's family was in a hurry to marry her off."

I tried to know more, but Ammi was vague. Her whole body seemed to shrink with every word she said about Shabnam and the man who followed her. She did not specify anything except that Abba and Shabnam talked before the wedding and Shabnam agreed to it. That Ammi, as the first wife, also agreed to it, in the hope that Shabnam might birth an heir to my parents' otherwise anonymous lives.

A few minutes later, everything went dark. The three-times-a-week power cut that started two months ago because a power plant was getting commissioned on the other side of the town, or that's what the newspaper claimed as the reason we were without electricity several hours in a day, almost every day.

When Ammi and I reached home, Abba was walking in the interior courtyard full of spilled foliage and birdcall.

"Where are you two coming from?" he asked and rubbed his forehead.

Ammi walked away without answering.

"Do you want me to get you an aspirin for your headache?" I asked.

He waved his left hand in dismissal. Behind him, the wrought-iron balcony wrapped in vines looked like a ghost. This house was built by Abba's father at the time of the British Raj. He was a clerk for an officer from the East India Company, and before the officer left for England, he gifted a piece of land to my grandfather. The house had five rooms, including a large living room and two bathrooms on the outside. A long rectangle of a kitchen like a dungeon. Abba renovated it with his savings and got a bathroom constructed between the two bedrooms.

•

During the power cuts, Ammi and I spent our evenings in the kitchen, dressed in sweat-soaked blouses and phirans, listening to Shabnam's moans and Abba shushing her, the heat emptying and filling them again. Ammi clenched her teeth, her face honest with heat and anger. At this hour, the front yard was a labyrinth of fireflies, their paths electric, a fanfare. When the lights came on the sparkle in the air reduced to ugly bugs, shivering, mating with their wiry legs and antennae.

•

"Is there a beauty parlor at a walking distance?" Shabnam asked me one day.

"What do you need?" I looked at her perfectly arched eyebrows, the bleached golden hair on her jawline.

"Wax my legs. It has been two months."

"I do it at home, it's cheaper."

"Your Abba gave me some cash." She paused, hesitating to divulge any more.

In the only ladies' salon in our neighborhood on the outskirts of Jammu, I watched the beautician waxing Shabnam's limbs until she pulled the curtain for a bikini wax. Ammi never allowed me to go to the salon except for a haircut every few months. I used a pumice stone at home to remove hair from my arms and legs. It left red bruises and bumps from rubbing too hard, since the hair never came off easy.

"No hair, he wants no hair," Shabnam whispered amidst her muffled screams. I wondered if silking the pubes guaranteed a boy. What if Shabnam delivered a girl?

On our way back, Shabnam kneeled on the dusty sidewalk, puked kebabs and rice, Ammi's curses and disdain, her garam masala. She puked Abba's cough, his outdated lust. I helped her get to her feet. Right away, the strays came and licked at her leavings on the pavement. We stopped by a tea stall to get some water.

"I crave a sugared lemon," Shabnam said, her face bleached, translucent with sweat, an acidic cloud that drifted from her mouth to my nostrils turning my face away.

•

The pre-monsoon heat swept us. Abba's knees were sore on the prayer mat, his hands wobbly in the air—Allah, Shabnam Salamat, in that order.

Ammi then. In the smoky tunnel of the kitchen. Between her fingers, garlic cloves peeled out of their skins, smooth, white, pungent. Ginger shredded into long thin threads. Green chilies split, their seeds like a choker along their length. On the sil-batta, Ammi crushed coriander leaves, chunks of onions, and the chilies into a fragrant paste for curry. She was at it for hours, starting from the morning, finishing up at noon.

Paneer chaman, rogan josh, khatte baigan served on the table, sweat-beaded Ammi standing next to the feast like an accomplished owner. But nothing stayed in Shabnam's belly except cramps, her fingers pressing a slight bump below her navel.

"You need to eat, Shabnam," Ammi would say, her voice stern then soft. "A son my only wish, all I'd ever ask from you." And Shabnam would recoil like a child seeking shelter and eat. Minutes later, she'd lean over the toilet.

In the mornings, when Shabnam felt hungry, Ammi poured her long falls of spiced salted lassi that she sipped quietly. For the rest of us, there was kehwa, fragrant with almond and cardamom. Sunlight thickened and the reign of koels and pigeons began, while our sounds were limited to chewing, or Abba clearing his throat and shuffling the pages of a daily newspaper.

Every other afternoon the greengrocers walked the roadside holding their oversized baskets on their heads. Their resonating cries, "Sabzi le lo," summoned Ammi. In those drowsy, hot hours, Shabnam would be in the bedroom reading a magazine or an old novel she brought with her in the red suitcase. After a long bargaining war, Ammi would agree upon a price, and the goods and money would exchange hands.

•

The monsoon hollowed the ground. Earthworms and leeches on the soaked concrete of the verandah, plump. The lights inside the house hissed and flickered. My head spun with the rot of Shabnam's frequent retching, so I carried a burning incense stick wherever I went and laundered every piece of cloth I could find. The air was full of strange scents: wet earth, detergent, rose incense, and vomit, all mixed up, nauseating like stale fish.

Often, Shabnam woke up in the middle of the night, and not to disturb Abba, she stepped out of their bedroom and sat on the stairs. On several occasions, I was awake listening to songs on the portable radio at the lowest volume because Ammi was asleep in my room. Together, Shabnam and I strolled on the terrace and watched the sparkling lights of the city turn off one by one.

•

When Shabnam miscarried, her wails gored the night. Abba stared at her as if saying, Stop crying with those stupid eyes. Stop scream-ing. Ammi and I washed the floors, slurred the blood into the drain. Pinned bleached sheets and mourning on the clothesline. Abba brought hakims: they examined Shabnam's pulse and prescribed herbal medicines and dietary restrictions. Light evening meal. Noth-ing chilled or cold. Preferably rotis and bottle gourd, squash. Once in a while khichdi. Ammi consulted a clairvoyant. He did a mental calculation based on Shabnam's and Abba's birthdate and time, and said that Shabnam's body attacked itself, her womb wasn't set correct, never would be.

Ammi started spending her mornings listening to discourses from pir sahib on an old cassette player.

Abba rattled the television set all day, but the screen stayed black. He concluded water puddled inside, ruined its wiring. The weary song of the ceiling fan broke the silence in the afternoons. Shabnam stayed in the bedroom, a giant mound of clothes on Ammi's once-immaculate floor, a slow river of tears in her cupped palms, her nose snotty. Occasionally, she walked out into the verandah, mumbling and nodding her head, her hand over her belly as if her fetus were still bobbing in it. Then she turned away and ran to her room as if answering her baby's wail.

Some days, Ammi uncoiled Shabnam's braids, combed her hair, oiled, and massaged her roots. From a distance, they looked similar with light salting their faces, keeping their grief lit.

•

After the monsoon left, the house smelled of dried milk, a can of stale, bitter almonds. Abba and Shabnam became a bad routine. Every morning, Shabnam walked and touched the walls, finally standing in the corridor with a pair of salwar kameez, a faded pink towel, her body shrunk, her eyes fixated somewhere between the floor and the ceiling while Ammi filled the bathroom bucket with hot water for Shabnam's bath.

Abba stayed on the diwan, his hookah repaired and filled again, the smoke settled on the ceiling like a ghost. Old Hindi film songs played on the radio. Its round metal dial reflected sunlight and threw colors onto his face. His low, drawling cough pulled something tight inside my stomach. He gazed at the walls, his eyes filled with a realization as if he had erred. Unaccomplished in having a son. And not loved. No longer by Ammi, never by Shabnam. The dog yelping on the street after someone had hit him with a stone.

•

It was during the Eid celebration that I saw Shabnam smile after months. She was talking to Abba's friend's son, Hassan, floppy black hair. When she came into the kitchen to help me and Ammi, she slipped her hand into mine and smiled. Her gaze transfixed me. Up close I saw a fleck of silver around each of her pupils. Heat rose between my legs like the sensation of hot kehwa down my throat on a cold, misty evening. Fluid, easy.

All this time, I thought to myself as I lay in my bed at night. I wasn't certain how such a thing would happen but the possibility of feeling her skin simmered me to madness. I looked up at the ceiling, watching the fan turn. My breasts shivered softly, my heart pulsed between my legs. As I came, I let out a slow cry followed by a gasp, the trailing edge of the sound making me warm and drowsy, but I wasn't ready to sleep just yet, when the thoughts of being with Shabnam lingered so closely. Headlights from the vehicles on the street momentarily lit the walls and the dresser of my room, the oval mirror white and smooth as an egg, and then darkened. My fingernail scraped below my navel, my desire wanting to be fed again. And again.

•

It became a norm to ignore my father, unless he cursed and shouted one of our names, asking for tea or hot water to bathe or a change of clothes. Sometimes he cried—first slow sobs then louder, begging Allah for a son even though we all knew he was sleeping by himself. Shabnam helped Ammi in the kitchen—washing and dicing vegetables, cleaning the meat from fat, soaking it in spices and yogurt. Once she stopped by my room and asked if she could borrow my red lipstick, my burnt-orange nail polish. I offered to paint her nails and she climbed on my bed with a girly shyness. I sat next to her, my knees folded, brushing against hers. My fingers trembled slightly as I painted her straight, even nails. She commented on the cleanliness of my space, breathed next to my ear. I mostly laughed or stayed quiet because I was afraid I would say something too frightening to forget.

When I bathed, I thought of Shabnam. Our bodies slippery with foam and want. In the late afternoon, she asked me to go out for a walk, I left everything and held her hand. It felt lighter than a pair of Abba's glasses. We strolled on the road that circled the valley. Birds landed on the railings. Two squirrels embraced. We climbed a lone flight of stone stairs to a scenic point. It was a beautiful day, and neither she nor I wanted to go home, where our routine was to stand in the kitchen for hours and stir the mutton gravy or wait for the baby potatoes to dum cook in a spicy curd-based sauce.

"I feel like a bird," she said and stretched her arms, imitating the flapping of wings.

"I know the feeling," I said, and interlaced my fingers in hers, and lowered her arm. She kissed my hand, and for the first time I felt the fear of losing Shabnam. Everything around me was so gentle I worried I would ruin it for looking at it too long. For wanting it too much. Walking back, we stood by a nursery where toddlers played. Shabnam watched them, her face rainbowed in the dusk. A man on a cycle, selling ice cream bars in flavors of mango and orange, circled us twice.

When we returned, our lips were red from licking the orange bars, sucking the wood stick as if it were a teat. The sun was ruddy on the pillow of sky. The birds had left. It was the happiest day of my life.

•

"What do you think of Hassan?" Shabnam asked one evening as we were climbing stairs to the terrace to pick up our clothes drying in the sun.

I looked at her. She pulled Abba's vests slowly from the clothesline as if they were frail like his body. The sun was at such an angle that everything glimmered in luminescence, the roofs of the surrounding houses spiked with crooked TV antennas, the fogged-up windowpanes, the pigeon droppings on our terrace. In the slanting light reflected from the windowpanes of another house, she looked like she was in a movie.

"I like him," she said, and giggled.

"Shh," I said, pressing my loud heartbeat with a heap of Ammi's petticoats to my chest. She whispered how she thought Hassan had beautiful hair and eyes. It reminded her of her grandfather's favorite dog, Roshan. Dark fluffy hair, eyes like coffee beans in a cloud of cream. I laughed at her description and squeezed her hand. It felt soft, boneless in desire. A part of me wanted her to go on so I would become a confidante, a part of me wanted to pull her into me, so she could replace Hassan's name with mine in her memory, but we ran downstairs with the smell of laundered cotton on our faces, warm with the last mean stretch of summer, a gentle confusion of our bodies against each other at the landing.

•

It was October when Abba's scooter collided against the railing on the road and he hit his head. Two days in the government hospital where he died of hemorrhaging. The men carried him away for a burial, his body wrapped in a kafan. I could not sum up how I felt. Perhaps my affection for Abba was lost in the past few months after Shabnam lost the baby. Perhaps I was only focused on Shabnam. Ammi's eyes were sore from crying, her throat roughed up like a hardened raisin. Twenty-eight odd years of holding the marriage together with Abba had stooped her shoulders. In all of this, Shabnam stayed quiet, her gaze settled on Hassan as he helped with Abba's body, occasionally meeting her eyes, a light smile escaping from the edge of his lips. I felt strangely satisfied and jealous watching them as I consoled Ammi.

I helped in the kitchen when Shabnam excused herself for a few minutes and disappeared for a couple of hours. I imagined Hassan jumping and crossing the connected roofs and coming down that vine into a small nook of garden shaded by bougainvillea, where Shabnam told me she waited for him. I imagined him caressing her cheeks, kissing her forehead and her neck, throwing her dupatta to the ground, affection and desire she didn't receive from my father. Ammi's eyes were drawn to the door at the slightest sound that resembled footsteps, but she never said anything.

Later, Shabnam would arrive, her hair stuck to the nape of her neck, her face flushed with satisfaction. At night after my mother slept, I'd ask details of her meeting with Hassan, I'd threaten to turn her upside down to see what secrets would fall. We'd doze off with our fists closed, holding the day's events in the palm of our hands. Sometimes I'd wake up when the pink feverish dawn would scatter in our room and I'd watch her slow-heart breathing, a wide turf of black hair on the embroidered pillow, her porcelain smooth toenails creeping out the blanket, the skin around them still pink from their recent encounter with the clippers.

•

Two months after Abba's death, Shabnam told me she was pregnant. The nausea, the rumbling of her stomach returned. Initially, Ammi looked skeptical whether Shabnam was carrying Abba's baby, but then she pretended she was. For her, there was nothing else to hold onto, so she described in detail how late at night, Abba sneaked into their bedroom and woke Shabnam to accompany him outside. How she heard their whispers despite the loud crickets, their shuffling on the old, narrow diwan in the living room, the muffled sighs, the silent release. How Shabnam tiptoed back to the bed and fell asleep while she, Ammi, cringed in the dim hours left till dawn, a scalding flash of her leftover marriage, the swallowing void of loneliness and shame.

"You didn't hear a thing, Ammi," I scoffed. "You are making this whole thing up and putting a lid of your pain on it to make it believable!"

"There are some things you can't fight against," she said, and shook her head as if she felt sorry for me because I wanted to be right rather than hopeful.

I asked Shabnam if she had talked to Hassan. If I could help them elope. Out of this town, out of this state, somewhere far away. Suspicious, she looked at me. "What are you saying? The baby's your abba's."

"No, it isn't," I protested.

Her cheeks flushed. She looked away for a minute and collected herself. Then she met my eyes. "You are going to have a baby brother," she said.

"How do you know it's a boy?" I said, and trembled in anger and sadness, not knowing what she was up to.

"Because that's what I owe," she said. "Coming," she yelled, and walked away as if answering my mother's call.

I wondered if giving birth to a boy was our deepest desire. If by demanding to know about the father of Shabnam's child, I was also doing the same.

•

For the next few months, Ammi was enthusiastically back in the kitchen making Shabnam's favorite dishes. Shabnam kept most of the food in. She rested, she smiled, she glowed like milk in moonlight. She slept in my mother's bedroom. There was a new TV—smaller, color, whatever my mother could afford with Abba's savings. The house was free of the stench of his tobacco, his bodily detritus, the electricity of his unrest and his obsession with news. It was tidy in the ways I found cold and uncomforting. No dried chai in the mugs. No frying pans caked with batter or eggs. No heap of washed clothes on the diwan. Abba's hookah wrapped in an old muslin and kept away in a steel trunk. I started looking for work, to stay out of home as much as I could.

Shabnam tried to talk to me, standing in the doorway of my room several times during the day. I don't know what I felt toward her—a growth of disgust followed by a space of indifference. Sometimes she dropped a pen, a newspaper, or a spoon in my vicinity and, struggling to bend, her eyes caught me watching. I almost ran to help her, and she almost thanked me, but we both continued on our own without either thing happening.

The new year decorations were still on the trees and the homes when I found a job in a grocery store. Pack, unpack. Check labels. Move things to shelves, remove things from shelves. Check labels. Replace, recycle, or throw. On my way back home, I walked slower to watch the lights come on in the houses on the hills. They flickered like lamps floating in the air. The river slapped against the rocks in the dark valley like an angry mother. The dirt around it slick and shiny. How many times I had been on this road, watching the steep slopes wondering if someone ever survived a fall, if the canopy caught their hearts, knotted it in their branches and leaves, until it went cold and purple and dropped like a shriveled berry.

Some days, I finished early and watched a movie playing at a theater half a kilometer away from the store. I didn't care what was playing, I just wanted to feel the dimness as the space around me dissolved and the slight commotion when the hall bulbs flickered back to light, rearranging everything as it was. Thrice, I watched the Hindi movie *Qurbani*, lip syncing to the songs. Zeenat Aman dancing in glitzy dresses with slits going up to her thigh. Her silky hair spread on her bare back. It made me forget the sourness I felt at home.

On evenings misted with the scent of saffron and cardamom tea, I rested in my room after work. White tube light numbed the air as Shabnam's voice overlapped Ammi's from the next room. I wouldn't guess what time it was until Ammi brought dinner to my room and asked about my day. Sometimes, lying on my bed, I'd see Shabnam walking slowly toward the bathroom, her belly pronounced even in the dim light of the corridor. Her sighs followed by my ammi's anxious response, "Sab theek?" I had a strong desire to shake Ammi's shoulders, grip hard into those sagging bones under the sudden gravity of affection for Shabnam, but I stayed where I was, motionless.

•

Over the next few days and weeks, I had restless dreams about Shabnam's baby—a boy with droopy eyes like Abba's, a flop of hair like
Hassan's. He cried when I tried to take him in my arms. Then he
crawled and followed me into my room and sat at the doorstep, holding my slipper in his hand, inspecting it. Once, he grew bigger, but
his face remained like a baby, he laughed with no teeth. We were
both inside what seemed like a womb, our bodies steeped in the in-
digo sap, drifting into darkness. From a faraway place, I could hear
birds, I could hear Shabnam's laughter. The sound felt as if coming
across the cartilage and muscles of the cage we were in. I dreamt of
Abba waking up in his grave, digging himself out. His mouth was
filled with dirt, so he gagged, keeping his finger pointed at Shabnam's
belly. One night I woke suddenly, frightened and lost, and flung out
my hand to hold onto something, the emptiness of my bed blotting
out the world.

•

Often, in the early hours of the morning, Shabnam got up to use the
bathroom. Sometimes she paused next to the door of my room, catching her breath, moaning, and awakened by the sounds I watched her
whispering something to herself, standing with the remaining darkness of the night, gathering her strength. Then she placed her palm
on the wall and moved forward. I waited to hear the running water
and know she was done before going back to sleep.

It had been raining for a few days and the roof was leaking. There
was water in the corridor next to the bathroom. Ammi handed me
rags and old towels to dry the floor. For several minutes, I stood still,
imagining Shabnam walking to the bathroom in the dark while water
pooled around my rubber slippers, touching my toes. Then I turned

around and returned to my room, the towels and rags dry on my arm. I am not sure why I did not dry the floor as instructed or chose that way to hurt Shabnam. Possibly I thought there was a chance that nothing might happen to her. For hours, the reflection of standing water stayed heavy on my eyes.

•

That morning when Ammi woke me up, she had blood on her hands. She pointed to Shabnam lying in the corridor, her cream salwar piled around her ankles, stained red. Her face turned toward me, her eyes wet and penetrating, her small triangle of chin shivering. She looked like the young girl I saw at her wedding, and in that moment, I remembered when I was in love with her, I could not recall when I stopped. I rushed to her, the floor slippery pink.

In the ambulance, Shabnam held my hand. I wiped her tears with the corner of my dupatta, the drool on the side of her lips. Outside, the blown glass sky dripped with crisp sunlight, coppered at the edge. On the side of the curved road, wildflowers lay on a carpet of green leaves like alms onto spread-open palms.

I squeezed her hand, and a bit of color came back to her cheeks. She released my fingers, eased by my compassion. She tried to turn her mouth up into a smile. At a distance, a shikara moved slowly across a lake, unstitching the water, the small waves like lines folding on themselves.

Ammi kept her eyes closed. A stream of tears touched the edge of her jawline, found a way down her neck into her blouse, soaking the cloth, her blood-streaked fingers advancing the tasbih. The lines on either side of her mouth softened by her expression of prayer. We went past the dirt roads, barking dogs, beams of sunlight on the traffic signals making them harder to see, accelerating and braking through a battery of horns and crowds, our progress slow and fitful.

In those moments, what wouldn't I give to go back in time and wipe the floor dry where she slipped, shattering that accusatory beeping of instruments around me, a guilt so complete implying something eternal and dreadful from which I could no longer hide.

Shabnam Salamat, I wanted to say, but enormously embarrassed at the weakness of my mind, a band of muscles tightened in my chest, my mouth went dry. The silence was harder to swallow, so much that my tongue began to ache and raw sobs bumped up my throat. Instead, my fingertips pressed on Shabnam's slim wrist as her pulse softened then dimmed while my back rocked with the motion of the van and my face squished against the cold window, squinting to see as far as I could.

BUBBLEGUM

THE GIRL HAS CREATED a bubble with 1/3 cup glycerin, 1/3 cup water, and 1/3 cup dishwashing soap after her third psychiatrist visit. Years ago, she was a perfect baby—a head full of black curls, big eyes, and a wide smile. After she turned five, something went wonky with her neurotransmitters. The doctor wrote a new prescription, but the girl didn't want to pop any pills. The bubble's supposed to last at least for a month because of all that glycerin.

The girl lives inside the bubble. It wobbles when the girl floats like a butterfly, like cotton candy. She has a crooked grin and her body behind the prism looks like an alien. She naps in child's pose.

Every evening, the girl rolls her bubble onto the porch, her horizon-bound gaze misted in the trapped air. Inside the house, her father sleeps on the sofa. He has Marlboro breath and sunken eyes; food from his last meal always shows between his teeth. There are toothpicks around him. He wakes up a few minutes before his shift at a convenience store. Her mother, a dry cleaner, eats and watches TV in the bedroom. She smells of kerosene.

Inside the bubble, the girl can hardly hear her parents arguing over food or finances. Sometimes they have company. Kids come around and touch the bubble. The girl winces, rolls away.

Until a week ago, the girl had a name. Now her mother calls her

Bubblegum, the cough in her throat thick with mucus. At night, her bedroom door opens a crack, and she sleepwalks toward the girl, puts on loud music and dances with her eyes closed, her tongue licking her lips like an animal craving for a treat, her singalong voice harsh and raspy. The girl zones out, imagines how the bubble looks from far above—a glass bead, a moon, a planet slipping on its axis—something you'd want to pick up and watch the rocking stillness inside it.

The girl tries to remember the list of words her teacher gave the last day she was in school, stories her mother never read at bedtime. She regrets not bringing the doll lying at the bottom of her toy trunk, the puppet her grandmother got from her visit to India—one with round, kohl-lined eyes and painted red lips, open, as if about to say something.

The bubble swells on the sides where the girl brushes her lips. Tastes sour. It has been a part of her for weeks, a sister now. She runs her fingers across the periphery and the bubble reflects her insides—a pair of drank-to-excess kidneys sitting on an inactive bladder, a brain cooked by pills behind the double doors of her eyes. She tries to catalog her organs, but the labeling is muddled. Pores and follicles are simply holes, the hair ready to sprout under her arms, between her legs, is trouble. She glances at her blood-soaked heart and a peanut-size uterus, slightly twisted butterfly-shaped lungs—hollow sacs everywhere. Then she leans back, wondering if she'd create bigger bubbles or split atoms when she grows up, if she'd need to impress others to find love. A fluffy moment before she realizes her feet are glued to the inner surface of the bubble. She moves her legs frantically—the bubble elongates sideways, tapers, and shrinks, but does not burst. The girl starts sobbing, tears falling, blood hammering in her temples. She hasn't known fear. She hasn't realized the bubble is a body, a space to hold everything that isn't pretty. Until now. She looks down at her toes. When she brings her head up, she catches a spectrum reflecting off the edge, filling rainbows in her eyes. They gleam and gleam.

THERE ARE PLACES THAT WILL FILL YOU UP

AFTER MY DAD SLEEPS, I open the back door. My mother pussyfoots into the kitchen. She's wearing a night-blue eyeliner and purple lipstick, looks like someone from the Anastasia commercial. I have only seen her once before today, chatted with her often. My dad claims she's a witch: once I start hearing her words in my head, my life as a normal person will cease to exist. But meeting her is a dare, a defiance. So I look for gaps in Dad's surveillance. Besides, she is my mother. It's weird to think that I know so little about her.

My mother pulls out a tissue from the box on the counter, dabs her eyes slightly covered by her curled bangs. "I'm so happy to see you," she whispers. She looks every bit human: unsure, full of enthusiasm, hungry for love, the corners of her mouth twitching as if she's about to say something but doesn't. I have imagined her often. Now face to face, I am drawn to her like lungs to air.

Together, we go through her latest Instagram posts. One photo of a mango grove has over a hundred likes. My fingers hover over the picture. "Not too far from here," she smiles, her ivory-colored painted nails clicking on the Corian. "There are places that will fill you up," she says, glancing at the ceiling, and I feel useless even though Dad has taken me with him on his business trips across Europe and Asia, to Turkey, to cruises, Disney World.

"Next week?" she asks before she slides open the patio door. Outside the moonlight falls across the grass, makes it look artificial. I put her address in Google Maps. The distance as per the blue line is walkable. I am certain that my dad has no idea she lives so close.

My mother says she loved Dad. It worked for a few years then it didn't. When he found out she was pregnant, he fought for my custody and won. Since then, she keeps bees in her purse. Whenever she opens the clutch, they crawl on her fingers, lace them with honey. She licks them clean, asserts that it's the sweetest love she has received in her life. Until now.

The next week, I skip school, walk to my mother's home. The trail to her home is lined with yellow and blue wildflowers; I make a bouquet on my way. She is waiting at the doorstep, her extravagance beyond endurance. I smell her lavender perfume, a whiff of veg korma and basil bread. As we sit to eat dinner, light streams in through the slits between the blinds and forms rectangles on the wooden floor, like windows to another world.

One evening, in her living room, my mother casts a spell, her eyes turned upward, moths lined up on her spine, stories in every rib. She says she can see the night braiding behind the sunset and all our previous lives. The spells rise around her like smoke, hover above our heads, faces in them: a tiger, a snake, an old woman, their faces changing, their faces the same, their eyes empty. "Every life is incomplete without a good death," she says and places her lips on my forehead. My body feels soft like a wet ground.

The next time I am at her place, I text my dad that I'll be studying and sleeping over at a friend's place. He asks a few questions before saying goodnight.

Deep in the woods, my mother brings me to a house that traveled everywhere because its owners were disabled. Boxy with a peaked roof. I sense the ghosts inside, but it feels clean, airy, full of hope. The wallpaper is a world map, pushpins on it, threads running across. She talks of a time when the old couple was still alive, sitting by the tall glass windows, waving as the house strutted by. She says if I'm quiet, I can hear them through the floorboards, in the pipes, the couple talking about the trips, the souvenirs, the skyline they brought back. We go in every room and come out of a different exit. "It's like love," my mother says. "You enter it in an obvious, grand way and crawl out an unexpected hole, slathered with suffering."

For the next few nights, I imagine living in the traveling house. I dream of sleeping next to my mother, breathing her magical air. I take a break from meeting her, not to get Dad suspicious. She messages me incessantly.

"Come."

"Just once. Come."

On our next nightly outdoor trip, my mother points to giant flowers glowing in the dark. She talks about the last monster she had known, a sea python several kilometers long, with colonies of flora and fish inside it. They ate away its skin, setting themselves free, not knowing that the serpent had kept them safe from the dangers of the waters. In the moonlight, she looks powerful, enigmatic, smells of darkness and salt, survival. We have picked up the pace, our shoulders are set, our strides long. We have so much in common. The bees in her purse buzz.

"At this hour?" I ask. "I thought they'd be asleep." The soft tendrils of the night mist wrap around our necks. She smiles and opens her purse. The bees scatter, get into her hair, on her face. They look like fingertips with a sour yellow light around them, their edges blurry, honey warm. I want to touch her, but she tells me to give up any suspicion before I do so, otherwise the bees will sting.

Back at home, my mother makes hot chocolate. She tells me how she met Dad, how he loved her kaftans and her tattoos, her glorious body, until he met someone else at his work, someone of his own kind. I watch her eyes turn pink. Outside the lightning fills the skeleton of sky. She lights a match and asks me to stand on the living room rug with orange and turquoise flowers, their centers dark like mouths. She does not drop the match even as the orange flame reaches her fingers. "It helps me focus," she asserts. "Do you know how you came to exist? These limbs, eyes, that mouth." She lights another match.

"No," I say, my knees knobby. I want to ask her if she sees herself in me. If I remind her of Dad. If we've been together in past lives, or separated, seeking each other. But I don't hear my words, I hear the clock in my ears, my heart synced up to it. I want to sit. I want to lie down.

"If you want," she says and caresses my hair, her fingers dark with soot, "we can live in that traveling house." In this light, her hair looks longer than before, her hand twitching like a lizard. "We can be in the woods every night, feel the cool mud under our feet, dig out rocks, catch luminescent bugs, live forever," she whispers, her breath a warm, moist draft on my face. She pinches my eyebrows, smooths my nose, looks closely at my face. I see the moons setting in her eyes, my dad's skin slowly tearing away, a world beyond it with stars across the periphery, serene lakes, groves of mango trees swaying in a tropical breeze. My body collapses and all I can do is hold to her words. All I can do is remember.

When I wake up, there is smoke outside. It wafts through the hallways of the house. My mother is in the backyard, burning something. I walk up to her, watch my schoolbag and my notebooks crumble in fire. Ink, words, vellum. "Cut loose from your past," she says, and presses my forehead with the palms of her hands. I feel her life line merging with my creases, the warmth of the red-yellow fire surrounding me like armor. When she moves away, tears well up in my eyes, form a line to my lips. They taste like honey.

Inside the house, I ask her if she slept. "Some nights, I don't," she says and continues pruning the indoor plants. A shingle falls off the roof, joining the simmering dark heap in the yard. "A part of us will be buried with what we just burned," she says and moves to the fridge, takes out peanut butter.

My phone vibrates in my pocket, three messages from Dad. I know he'll figure it out soon, so I look at my mother, she acknowledges as if she can read my thoughts. Her eyes are bright and joyful. I start texting. The words pop into my head, not my own, but convincing, better than anything I can think right now. Sentences. Reasons, well-articulated, humming in my ears. One after another like ants in a line, heads bent, orderly.

ONE MILKY WINDOW

WINTER NIGHTS WHEN DELHI is shrouded in dense fog. The other side of the bed is neat, uncomplicated. Your message on my phone: *My flight is delayed.*

I get up in the pale blue of the night, clots of dreams behind my eyes. A hunchback appears where there had been your brown jacket on the chair. I walk in the verandah until I reach the edge of the balcony and back to my desk. The screensaver on my laptop has changed from mountains to oceans to volcanoes and craters. Places we have visited in what seems like another century and brought the skyline back, fitted it in this bone-white house. The flowers in the vase have wilted to mark the passage of this week without you. I wish I had more words to describe the loneliness, the white shredded night around me. You smile from our honeymoon picture on the wall. A sharp jawline merged with my hair in the wind, your eyes closed, my mouth open. I lower my breathing; you are here, and you are not here. Sometimes I wish to hit my head and start all over.

•

"Let's get out this weekend," you say and light a cigarette. In the dim lighting of our living room, your eyes look darker. Thick maroon drapes pulled away, the moon swings low, one milky window between us. Your hand sits loosely on my thigh. "Somewhere in the mountains," you say, and inhale deeply, pass the cigarette to me. A whiff of clove-flavored smoke mixed with your aftershave. I want to believe you. Our eyes meet for a flash. "Let's just stay here," you retract, and raise your hand in dismissal.

"Come on." I make a soft sound of a reaction. "Let's go to the mountains."

"It's a busy month." You speak gently, as you would to a spooked pet.

My jaw tightens. I think of things to say, and I settle on staying quiet, tears caught in my lashes. An old wine stain shines on the rug, brightens the pain.

•

We met five years ago in a conference, Hyatt's ugly ballroom in South Delhi, a part of the city I was unfamiliar with. I saw you from across the room and thought I knew you. We sat at the bar, and I complained red wine always makes my lips dry. You drove me back to my hostel at the other end of the city. I was finishing up business management, you were an associate at a law firm. The next time, we drank with your friends, then one evening in your apartment until light came through the window.

The first time we had sex, you knew what to do with my wrists, how to follow my moving body and come up with a response. Stained sheets. The edges of the room blurred in the corner of our eyes, our bodies gutted, our hearts full.

I watched you in the arms of a deep-drunk sleep. A part of your forehead bright, shining. A moon in the dark sky of your face, an impermeable world. I pressed on your skin. You grabbed my finger in your sleep and we flew high, trembling in our dreams, love locked.

If I had to sum up my affair with you, I'd say: you made me

laugh to all the bad jokes on WhatsApp. Both when I thought you were in love with me and when you weren't.

We got married in October. Just before Diwali. We coupled fiercely in our bedroom, in the kitchen, in our balcony at night. In between our consummations, we laughed and passed around the beer and wine bottles. I came to yearn you more each day.

On our honeymoon, we went to Shimla. From our cottage windows, sunlight glinted off the Himalayan snow caps, drilling holes on the sheets covering our bodies tangled like braids. We went drinking tea and eating stuffed parathas at dhabas, saying iloveyouiloveyouiloveyou and exhaling puffy clouds from our mouths, rubbing our hands together. Once you bribed an attendant to get into a five-star hotel restaurant where only residents were allowed. We sat awkwardly in the coffee shop and ordered black forest pastries. When the waiter asked our room number, you said you were staying in the presidential suite. He packed coffee and sandwiches on our way out. Outside, I clung to you like a child lost in a fair. We sat on a park bench and ate, the potato filling in the sandwiches stuck between our teeth. We ran on the winding roads, called out each other's names, the echoes caught in the valleys like memories.

•

When my sister calls, it's evening. She moved out of Delhi two years ago. Unsafe, she claimed—too much traffic, everyone yelling, drowning you in noise. I look at the pigeons outside my window while she imitates the Punjabi landlord of the house where we grew up. We were not rich, but we made it work. "Remember the stories Mom used to read to us?" A girl shyness and excitement in her voice. "Mm hmm," I say and close my eyes. Those cold nights in a rajai pulled up to our chins, our mother's soft, husky voice.

Fog misted on our windows in the mornings, the chilled bathwater on our naked bodies. Later in the day, the sky wickedly luring, an unbelievable tarp of blue.

•

The sky is a mess of clouds when I go for a run. The layer of smog like a giant spaceship prevents the sunshine from permeating our skin. Prevents anyone from talking to us from another world. Is that vague pain on my left side a sign to fuck you or an organ spoiling? Will I be a mother soon? Will I be as good as I want to be? It hurts but I keep going, past the milkmen and shrill-voiced greengrocers, orphans sleeping under the bridge graffitied with slogans from political parties, piercing the light frost across Delhi's chest, as if it's supposed to reveal a heart, shivering, gray-blue on the edges, waiting to be embraced.

•

Over the weekend, you spend most of your time in the study and we end up visiting Chandni Chowk. The old charm of the capital dripping in syrup and curry from top to bottom, familiar call of hawkers. On our way back in an Uber: traffic with a side of mashup Bollywood songs. The sugar settling in my stomach, your light beard poking my cheeks. I want to stop time, ask the driver to pull over to the side of the road and stay until the traffic dissipates. I run my finger on your shoulders, your hands until you smile and withdraw. We weren't always like this—once we had kissed all the way to our home. Ahead of us, the brake lights flicker like laser dots pointing, crisscrossing rays trying to connect with someone, somewhere. We stay quiet, trying to outride the noise as if alone in the space we occupy, alone in Delhi throbbing around us, my light sweat like a mouth on my chest.

"We should try IVF," you say, and smooth the crease on your khakis.

•

On New Year's Eve, the fog leaves us. I call you at work to thank you for the flowers you left by my bedside. You say you have made reservations at a Japanese restaurant in Connaught Place for the evening. A thin ray of sunlight falls at my feet. I glance at the bouquet of lilies and a coupon for an hour-long ASMR session. I sulk at the number of days you're going to be away on business, from me, from us, in exchange.

•

My ASMR therapist whispers to imagine countless rose petals falling from the sky, filling light in every cell of my skin. I feel her breath, her touch so light that my body relaxes and blooms, expands and expands with the want to cry.

On my way back, pink electricity mauls the sky. I pull the unusual, wet afternoon apart by tearing fresh garlic bread. Musk in the air, in my mouth. Delhi, loose between her legs, drenched and sexy, calling out to her lover.

I am searing, I want you to swallow me whole.

•

The first IVF cycle takes about three weeks. Medications, blood tests, and ultrasounds. Cramping. My breasts are tender, sore. My gut constipated. Like breaking ground to construct a new town. Pouring foundation, metal beams to support the structure, except that it doesn't work.

"It takes multiple tries," the fertility expert says.

"Do you have kids?" I ask.

"Yes," she says and smiles.

After the second try at IVF, you take me out to Janpath, the street bazaar. A riot of colors too wild to focus, branches heavy with singing koels. A slosh in my belly, my body amplified by hormones. Cells tumbling, figuring out their biology, geometry, finding an opening. I try different dupattas and scarves around my neck like picking crayons from a box. Teal, salmon, gold, rose, magenta. When you bend down next to me, I study the curve of your hips, your damp, electric fingers picking up a dupatta, and try to come up with a name for the color of your skin, porous and bright.

Ahead of us, a group of monks, their red robes and shining heads, little suns. I want to ask them how to meditate, how to let go the needs of a body, how to not think about leaving a legacy. You click a picture. Cerulean skies, newborn skin of March, a yellow euphony.

·

In the distance, police sirens are at work. Moths surrounding the streetlamps visible from our windows. Buzzing, birthing, dying. Stray dogs barking, calling out to mate. Delhi illuminated with want. *Are animals lonely? Are cities lonely?*

I hear you come through the front door. You say you want to smoke but you won't, we should be healthy parents. I notice a gray curl above your left ear, the way it sits, delicate, like a new leaf, and I forget where I am.

·

I prop pillows on the bed to support my slightly grown belly. We are wearing May and the heat wave of Delhi. You put your arms around me. I hold your face. Feeling tender. You talk about baby names, a new paint on the walls, your travel for the year, your eyes staring at the wall behind me. I move my hands away from your face and press on the startling firmness of your shoulders, but you don't seem to notice, and I realize the span of years in the space between us, a knot of flesh, the waning fibers of love. I start rubbing your back, feeling your beautiful muscles as if I am a ruin already, as if I want to take root in you, as if I don't know what to do with all this hankering in me, while you keep talking and looking away, far, far from this moment, out of reach.

COW'S TONGUE

SOMEONE HAD LEFT A cow's tongue on our doorstep, the flesh dark pink, a row of flies on it like the line of hairs on Papa's chest. The stench was dense—my mother's mouth at the end of the morning lining curses all the way to the front door. Our maid brought a newspaper and swept the tongue onto it with a broom. The flies rose in the air, annoyed.

Before the verandah was swiped clean with milky phenyl water, I got a brief glimpse of the tongue. In the backyard, I was kissing my neighbor, Akbar—my tongue deep in his mouth, sucking his Lucknow tehzeeb, the sparse beard on his cheeks tickling my chin until I heard the commotion, the sharp voice of my mother calling on all the Hindu gods.

"Hey Ram," she yelled, "who could do this to us?" I heard her panicked steps approaching the kitchen, her long sighs filled with rage and frustration.

"Please." Akbar held my arm. "I have cigarettes." In the background, my mother called my name. "I will be back soon," I said and pushed his hand away.

Later, Akbar described how his ammi would have cooked the cow's tongue. Spices, yogurt to marinate, a slow roast. He swiped his tongue over his lips.

"Shh, we cremated the tongue, the broom, and the newspaper. A local priest performed a cleaning ritual," I whispered. Akbar laughed at the last part, a little rueful, his tall bulk listed against the brick wall. The street ahead of us was empty at this hour, the heat appropriate for June. We passed the cigarette to each other, the smoke curled in front of us like a fresh ghost. Then Akbar pulled me in, blew into my mouth. My lungs filled with a heady vapor.

"I wish you had a personal phone," he said. "Then I'd call and whisper love songs into your ear." Akbar with this tattoo of a flame on his upper right arm, mostly covered under his white kurta. Akbar with a tang of mutton masala on his finger pads, Akbar with slim curved ribs that bent like a spring as he kissed my neck. After he let go, I collapsed, the smoke escaping from my mouth one wing at a time—a bird.

•

During the month of Ramadan, I saw Akbar once during the day. I brushed his lips with mine. "Not when I'm fasting." He pushed and left me with those words. Shafts of neon-orange July light leaked through the branches of the mango tree in my backyard and over the hours melted into a soft dusk, just when it was time for him to open his fast. Arabic murmurs rose from his house. I had an urge to pull out a mat and sit in front of my favorite Lord Krishna and press my palms together in a prayer.

Another day it was only 10 a.m. and I was sweating a lot. Leaning against the brick wall where Akbar and I used to make out. Butterflies staggered in a nearby bush. A pre-monsoon mist haunted the road ahead of my eyes. I turned my head every time the leaves brushed against the window, as if someone were walking toward me. I waited for him and felt my mind drifting away to a place somewhere in the small of my back. My fingers traced his name on the uneven wall, scratched my palm.

•

When Akbar's ammi invited us for Eid, my mother refused to attend. "It was someone from their family who threw the cow's tongue on our doorstep."

Papa shook his head. "We'll go," he declared.

I shaved the hairs on my arms and legs, armpits, down from my navel. I used a curling iron—my hair like silk ribbons, bouncy on my cheeks and back. I knew Akbar's cousins would be there, especially Atif. Atif who winked at me on several occasions, Atif who was muscular with boring brown hair. Atif who would gladly pay attention to me.

I plucked the hairs between my eyebrows and wore a tight golden blouse with a green, sparkling ghaghra, bare midriff.

Inside Akbar's home, I walked upstairs, waited at the door of his room. Downstairs, my Hindu parents mingled with their Muslim neighbors, being civil to each other's customs and traditions like the past ten years since we moved in. Akbar was at the window, watching birds landing on the mango tree. When he turned around, he took me in his arms. I forgot about Atif. I kissed him and his lips were coral.

Above his backyard pool, the sky hung, cinnamon-smudged and Lucknow pure; flushed, frowning, galaxies in water. A shy red sun dipped into the horizon.

"You know we cannot be together, sweetheart," Akbar said. Annoyed, I swatted his lips as if a mosquito had landed on them, even though I knew the truth—different religions, customs, traditions. My parents would die of shame, so would his. Blood rushed to my cheeks. I struggled to form words, so I looked away. He came close, nibbled my ears. Then he said my name. It boomeranged off my insides.

When I was ready to leave, Akbar gave me an audiocassette, a recording of his favorite Bollywood songs. "This is your Eidi," he said.

At home, I closed my eyes and listened to it. Songs from Hindi movies, ghazals, some reciting poetry from Faiz, Iqbal, Ghalib.

As if you are with me, just when

There is no one else around me.

•

The next time I saw Akbar was at his engagement to Rukhsana, his distant cousin. Her eyes hazel, her mouth wide, her thighs in the sharara like trunks of the banana trees. Her anklets rang, the hem of her dress bumped over the floor as she walked—not too fast or slow—and sat next to him. Akbar wore an embroidered sherwani, sleeves rolled up to his elbows in the way I liked. Akbar smiled and greeted his relatives, shook hands. The love-lacked look that scored his face. He looked grown up, distant. Rukhsana pinched her waist to adjust her dress, quirked an eyebrow. Was she so much better than me—being Muslim and beautiful, someone who'd cook a cow's tongue whereas I'd cremate it even though I'd find it absurd?

When Rukhsana hugged me as Akbar's neighbor and friend, I don't know why but I wanted to shake her, slip her out of the party and teach her everything Akbar enjoyed. I wanted to touch that mole on her left cheek and wipe that bit of lipstick smeared on her side tooth. I was feeling so kind toward her I felt I could not be trusted.

The mango tree looked like a dragon in darkness. "Sweetheart," Akbar said, pushed his tongue inside my mouth. Something rustled in the tree. I led his hand inside my blouse, between my legs, his skin warm as the soupy night. The lights in our homes turned off one by one. A mist illuminated their outlines. In the distance cars honked, fat drops of occasional rain tapped on our heads. Later, we cleaned each other with old newspapers in a pile for kabadiwala, a scrap collector. Moonlight leaked out of us.

It was past midnight when I showered, my bones taut like the elastic of my PJs. Tucked in bed, I thought of Rukhsana slipping a ring onto Akbar's finger. Their heads joined together by their elders, the blessings for a lifetime. Then I imagined Akbar naked in my backyard a few hours ago.

•

Mid-October, when Akbar and Rukhsana got married, I danced and got drunk with his friends who hid their liquor glasses in the trunks of their cars, their heads bobbing like microwaved popcorn I've seen in television ads. The loud music hollowed the night, his home lights whirlpooled. After the ceremony, Akbar and Rukhsana joined us, and she kept falling behind to catch his moves. But she had all the time in the world to synchronize with him. On the other hand, I stayed close to Akbar, our torsos sewn, our arms buttoned, our bodies shuddered along an ethereal curve. How musky his hair smelled at the sideburns, Old Spice aftershave lingering on his chin. We had finished ten beers. *Remember this touch, remember this move. Remember this street, this time. Remember this feeling.* High on pride and foreplay, we continued until our laughter was harsh and our throats stung. Until I realized I needed to go because my head was spinning, my body dry heaving.

I walked past the bride, her eyes flushed with anger and tears as I tried to smile at her. It was late, everything blue, violet, as if a carnivorous flower opened in the sky, its dark outer shell revealing the softer insides—the frilled edges, a row of curling tentacles. I knelt by the edge of the driveway flecked red with the flaming hearts of the gulmohar tree and puked the dinner and alcohol, the warmth rising from inside and leaving in a stream until my insides were empty, dry, and coarse like a cow's tongue.

TORNADO, FALLING

AFTER THE TORNADO, our hearts are stretched like Tennessee, our ears pointed in the direction of the wind. We have been sucked in the funnel; we have been spat. I carry my newborn screwed to my spine, his tongue licking the skin over my heart. I have gotten used to the weight. Our crumbled house fits into our palms. In my dream, I knock locked doors.

Before the tornado: my lover and I barely slept all night, the newborn kept waking us up. My lover pulled up his pants every time he picked up the newborn and brought him to our bed. Honey pink, the baby's gaze, his irises the color of upturned soil. We only had moments to stare at each other, to fall asleep again, a little dampness under our eyes, where fragrant plants could take root.

I think of the half-eaten cake in our fridge, imagine its crumbs falling off my mouth, like people thrown off the funnel. My dry mouth stays wide open like a dustpan.

As I pick through our belongings, my arms seem longer than usual. I am looking for the postcard my father sent last year before he passed away. It seems my waist has grown overnight, as if holding onto loss. My baby presses my insides like plucking something. I want to bring him out in sunlight, sing him our favorite song. But gray clouds are stuck above us, the space in between filled with a loud horror of things flying, crashing, an isolated emotion of fear.

My lover seems slimmer, hungrier. The funnel has upset his organs, changed his priorities. There is a desert in his eyes, his dark hair, long and shaggy, hanging around his face. Sad, beautiful. Sometimes he gives me a sour look. I bring him a water bottle; he stares at it for a long time. "This is the end," he says, and returns it to me. I stroke his hair. We used to play frisbee, we used to run somewhere here. Our neighbors are standing in their yard, or what used to be, their faces upward to the bare cloudy ceiling. It's impossible to explain how much I miss the walls.

I can see the stretch of my life ahead. My son growing up thinking everything is so goddamn difficult. Over time, I know we'll grow apart. I want to think of ten different ways my life would have been worse—illness, drugs—but I can't. My chest constricts. I just want to outlive this mess; I don't want to outlive love. A phone rings. They are talking of damage, compensation. It will take weeks, months to recover. I know everyone in this world is dying but it seems it's just us for now. A giant shadow passes over our heads, the blades whirring, a funnel rising then falling. Whipping wind. I hear my name and look around. There's nowhere to go.

The newborn cries. My breasts are full and hurting. When he sucks on them, his lips are lined with dust.

OB-GYNS I LOVED (IN RANDOM ORDER)

I SCHEDULED MY APPOINTMENTS with Dr. White in the afternoon because all the examination rooms faced southwest. She'd come in with her phone, which I think wasn't appropriate during a patient visit, but I loved to watch her standing next to the window, a halo around her head, biting her lip, and I knew she was sexting because she'd sigh before closing the app and her blue eyes would be glazed over. "So, sweetie, what brings you in today? Again?" A smirk on her lips, her neck tilted to her left side, a blue vein shining in a sunbeam. Bubbles rising in the pit of my stomach.

I'd make up something—vaginal dryness or burning, or a heavy period, moodiness. "Uh-huh," she'd say while guiding my legs into the stirrups and inserting her gloved finger, sometimes with a gel, sometimes without. "This might make you uncomfortable, sweetie, but we're just about done." Her nasally voice, a long thread of song pierced through my body. Once, she kept her finger in for the whole minute (saying she sensed a growth), but I knew she felt something for me too. "Looks good in there," she'd say and wink, pull her gloves off.

I was recently divorced and dating a man—he never went completely hard for me, but took me to Four Seasons, bought me a Coach purse and Chanel boots, so I didn't break up with him until a year later when I got custody of my kids. One night, he said, "I love you," before dropping me off at my apartment, so I told him about Dr. White and what I'd like to do to her. "Lick her boobs while my finger's drilling her, watch her cum pool in the palm of my hand." His dick rose like a fifteen-year-old staring at a topless picture of his favorite model. A few months after we broke up, we ran into each other at a mall. I got some lingerie and snakeskin boots and he tagged along. "Send me pictures," he whispered in my ears as we waited in the checkout line, his scruffy semi-beard tickling my cheek. I couldn't help but laugh. In a dark parking lot corner, we kissed for over half an hour, our clothes crinkled, damp underneath our moving hands. I could feel his hardness on my thigh through his khakis. Something that excited me, something I was happy to discover as if he was someone other than the man I used to date. At his place, he fucked me with his shoes on, and though it was remarkably satisfying with the kissing and biting, the right amount of slow and fast, I was surprised how little I cared. In some weird way, it gave me the confidence to ignore his future texts, or rather, pay attention to them whenever I wanted to.

Years ago, Dr. Blackwood in Allentown, PA, delivered my son. He was tall, patient, probably a decade older than me. I was twenty-seven. After six weeks of my pregnancy, when I went for consultation in his office, I saw a picture of his wife and three kids. Blonde, pale, all of them. Perfect teeth. A picture of him on the tennis court, his calf muscles taut like Pete Sampras. How his eyes seemed to take in all there was. Wise. A statue of Ganesha on his desk. "Are you a religious man?" I asked.

He shrugged and picked up the copper idol. His wrist was slim, all that power in the backhand. "My wife got this from her trip to India."

Dr. Blackwood's fingers were wide, they covered my breast while he pressed on the edges. My nipples rose in the soft air-conditioner air and at that moment, I wanted my boobs to be bigger, fuller, so he could feel more. "Any pain or discomfort?" he'd ask, and I could hear the crack in his voice. I imagined the scent of his body as he lay in his bed, his fingers on his wife's navel, slipping down, how he made her cry in pleasure in the early hours of the morning, her legs opening like a lantern wanting to be lit on the edge of darkness. Or what if he was a passive top like my husband? Nah.

Close to full term, when I got into the hospital, after a day and a half, Dr. Blackwood waited a whole forty minutes for me to push my son, before he used a vacuum since I was tired after a long labor and could no longer push for more than a second or two. I always imagined doctors led the healthiest lifestyle, until years later I found out that he died of cancer in his late forties. I googled and called the number of his clinic—it wasn't his voice, of course, a woman's, but it gave me a sense of closure.

I must admit all the OB-GYNs I met did not thrill me. There was a woman in southern Philly, her office west of the Schuylkill River, who'd never look me in the eye. Such a turnoff. She'd stand next to me listening to my heartbeat and I'd hear her stomach rumbling, and a sound as if she were about to burp. Her hair greasy, parted in the middle, her voice tremulous while asking questions with simple Yes/No as answers. I wondered if she felt anything. Anger, arousal. If someone ever made her cum properly. I watched her lips move, whispering to herself as she inserted her fingers in me. Perhaps she was praying, perhaps cursing. It was hard to say since her expression always remained the same. Then we moved to New Jersey and there was Dr. Phillip—short, bald, and golden-framed glasses. Every visit, he talked about the weather and licked his lips frequently like a snake. Inside me, his finger felt as if there was a sharp nail at the edge of his glove, scratching my insides. He'd snicker before leaving the room—forgetting my name, then looking at my file and pronouncing it wrong. "These Indian names are so complicated," he'd go on with a sneer. Prick.

Three years before my son was born, Dr. Uni delivered my daughter. White shirt and suspenders; smelled like disinfectant. His office was in an industrial complex and there was a steady drone of grinding, whirring—a machine at work. After waiting for a few minutes in the reception area, the sound would hang around the edges of my ears while Dr. Uni talked about conspiracy theories from moon landings to solving the hunger issue in developing countries as the heartbeat of my baby echoed in the room. "It's going to be a boy," he predicted, and I don't know what I felt for him. Uni was his nickname—no one knew his full name and age. Google was just becoming popular.

My first love was a gynecologist named Dr. Surya who performed my D&C after eight weeks. It was in the first year of my marriage and my husband never wanted a child so early. I had morning sickness and frequent spotting. Dr. Surya held my hand, rubbed the edges of my fingers while I sobbed. Up close, she smelled of sandalwood and garam masala, and I felt I was a needle pointing home—how soft her touch, not shitty like my husband's that always felt prickly, his eyes zoned out as if he wished he were somewhere else. Afterward, I watched the fluorescent air buzzing in the surgery room while the suction cleared my womb, the blurred lines of Dr. Surya's frame as I went in and out of consciousness, my legs apart, the invisible beating between us.

MOTHER, GALAXY X

My mother is talking to a stranger, a bald man with lukewarm brown eyes wearing a silver jacket, his legs stretching out of his shorts, gnarled like tree roots, a gadget on his wrist, changing colors, hissing. He claims to be from Galaxy X. My mother laughs it off. She introduces me as her little sister. I ask her if we can go home. "Hush now," she says, "our friend is taking us to dinner." The man's eyes turn to red dots like lasers.

"Sure," he says.

The sky is a shade of stormy gray: the color of an old wound. There is the usual chatter around us, people talking on their devices, indifferent. There's something unsaintly about the man, the way he's watching us when he's speaking, and when he isn't. *Why is he here? Why is he talking to us, taking us to dinner?*

We enter a Chinese restaurant and order dumplings. My mother puts tiny pieces of food in her mouth as if she is a bird. I look at the last piece in the plate and when the man offers it, I grab it. We have been living on cereal and cheese sandwiches for over a week. My mother unzips her hoodie, runs her fingers through her hair, bends to pick up something that doesn't exist, trying hard to be likeable. Her voice is bright, joyful. They talk about the weather, their favorite actors and movies, striving to be romantic. He seems to know a lot

about us, the Earth, the way we are consumed with pride and shame.
There is an Asian couple in a corner, three rows of empty furniture between us. The waitress is staring at the main door, turning
her face toward us at every little sound we make. The man yawns
and there's a sparkling cloud around us. My mother gets up and sits
next to him. They start whispering to each other, slowly moving to
the rhythm of a faint music. For years, finding a man has been an
obstacle course my mother has not been able to complete. Right now,
in this light, she looks desirable, threads of fog in her hair, slowly
disintegrating, a cosmic event. I can see the man's hunger, the way he
is pressing his arm against hers, shutting his eyes as if charging them
up, as if to handle the heat between them.

We gulp the noodles slick with chili oil. "My throat is on fire,"
the man laughs, the sharp noise scratching my ears. He asks me
about school. I say I'm in high school and I have a lot of friends,
even a boyfriend. He nods his head and glances at my mother. She
starts describing an off-shoulder velvet dress she'd seen in an upscale
shop a few days ago. I close my eyes and imagine the texture of the
dress from my mother's description. For a moment, she is a princess,
drapes of red satin flowing all over her body. Soft and abundant like
space. Abundance and joy, my mom's face emerges like an evening
sky, satellites circling around her, making a tiara. Glimpses of stars
that once were. She looks like she's been waiting. And she may have
a chance this time, even though I think he's weird, no matter which
corner of the universe he's from.

I'd only believe if he's able to show us a moon or a sun different
than ours. In the background, I hear him asking her to make a list of
things she likes, the stuff she'd like to take with her on a journey with
him. Want translated to calligraphy, my mom, an earthly, starving
female converted to a potential slave. Or an experiment. I open my
eyes: the man and my mother are kissing, their illuminated bodies

lifted, stars falling around them. I want to stop her but it's the most beautiful thing in the world, first distance, then distant, and then memory. Stopping her would mean slowing down her ecstatic heart, turning her cold, alone and safe, tied to the gravity once again.

I call out her name, and the letters chafe before bursting into a million specks.

IT RAINED THAT DAY

SALMA OPENED HER EYES. She smelled fried oil in the air. Past the sliding window, an earthen lamp flickered on the sill, ready to go out with the first light. It was going to be another day with the storm clouds stacked up, circling the city. Wasim, her younger brother, who lay next to her, rubbed his eyes.

"Go back to sleep, Wasim," she whispered.

"Why are you up?" Wasim touched her hand and moved his legs, pushing the sheet away. Outside, the clouds collided, and a jagged silver beam lit the sky.

"Are you excited?" He blinked quickly, his eyeballs still heavy with sleep. "You're getting married and going to Dubai." He motioned with his arms and mouth, mimicking the liftoff of an airplane.

"I am...yes, of course." Salma touched his cheeks and slowly let her fingers drop over his little hands, lightly squeezing them. A dog howled in distance.

"I'm going to miss you. I wish you could take me with you." He came closer and touched her forehead with his. "Is Sheikh Abdullah fifty-five years old? You are only twenty-five. That is..." He started counting and stopped. "Wait, he is almost Abba's age."

Salma felt like vomiting. It felt as if the number went up and down her throat. The sky lit up again, followed by a clap of thunder making the walls tremble. It started drizzling and the lamp went out with a soft hiss. She kept a hand on her mouth, almost gagging on her bile.

"I have to help Ammi and get ready." She stumbled up and straightened herself, unwilling to process her anxiety any further.

She pulled the curtain that served as the bathroom door and stood by the stained glass of the window. Water running on glass looked like crisscrossed perforated lines. Like the women in slums— dark, young, bored, smiling, grumpy-faced housewives accompanied by their enthused, agile husbands and children walking through the mud, soot, and sweat, their hands pushing to make space for themselves. She cast her gaze around and the sick feeling returned. For at least a few days, she had indulged the fantasy of a better life elsewhere, away from this choked neighborhood that had been burnt, bent, and drowned and then emerged with multitudes of men and women as if nothing had happened. Yet today she focused on the smell and sound of the stale water in the flushes, taps, and rusty drains. The ditches that always overflowed during the monsoon and brought the water inside with dirt and earthworms, closer to their beds, stove, and clothes. The turns they took to sleep and eat. The odd-shaped trunk of the mango tree at the end of the alley, crowned with extravagant foliage and sour mangoes. Pieces of her home. Then she imagined the airplane soar, the straight-backed air hostess leading her to a seat made of the softest fabric, serving her food and drinks, flying away from the noise and shock of a slum.

Her father's snores traveled through the heavy air. In the past few years, her growing shadow had horrified him. Either it was her dark complexion and ordinary features or the money he was unable to give as a dowry to the groom and his family, but any decent match refused to come her way. There was a rumor that any girl who was unable to find a husband was forced into prostitution by the local mafia. During the day, Abba sat on the same one armchair, his feet stuck to the ground as if the weight of the earth pulled him down and buried a part of him. At night, he stayed up staring at the ceiling fan, unsure what to do except revolve at the same place, only slower. Sometimes, he fell asleep, cried and woke up with a scream. He refused to leave home until his stepsister and Salma's aunt brought a proposal from an old, wealthy sheikh from Doha who was looking to marry a young woman. Reluctantly, he agreed.

When Salma entered the kitchen, her mother's hands were white with dough. She stood at the door, watching a web in the corner, its shimmering threads holding a spider. She smelled the kerosene. A few raisins surfaced in a half-filled bowl, looking like dead bugs.

"Why aren't you ready?" her mother asked and started coughing. Humidity made Ammi's asthma worse. Covering her mouth with a muslin scarf wrapped around her head, she continued to fry squares of bread, arranging them on last Sunday's *Mumbai Mirror* to drain excess oil, avoiding eye contact.

"May I?" Salma asked, looking at the sweet treat, her hands trembling at the same frequency as her voice.

"Just one," replied Ammi. "Here, take these earrings, too." She cautiously removed two golden rings from her ears. Without the ornaments, Ammi's ears appeared as large lobes of skin, hanging without purpose. As Salma touched Ammi's hand, their eyes met.

"It is the cough. My eyes are runny all the time. Go and get ready." Ammi turned her back to Salma. "There is a strip of sandalwood soap in the gap between the sink and the wall." Ammi's voice shook for a moment before it steadied.

Inside the bathroom, Salma touched her face and wondered if she should run away. If Abdullah would never let her see her family again. If she should walk on the road chosen for her until she found her own. If she'd die without knowing the man she deserved. The

endless questions fell on the ground like the rain outside, with nowhere to go. She held the tap, jerked it and wept.

"Salma, are you all right?" Abba's trembled voice seeped through
the curtain. In the faint light that peeked between the edge of the
floor and the swaying cloth, she could see more feet joining Abba's.

"Yes, Abba, I'm fine." Salma swallowed the hiccup and turned
the tap. It gurgled, sucking in all the air before spitting water. Outside it rained in torrents. Salma thought of things she'd do with Wasim on their bus ride to the airport. They'd make figures out of yellow
sponge plucked from the torn seats, eat the sweet bread together and
make fun of the old, bald bus driver. And when he would rest his
head in her lap, she'd sense his heartbeat under her palm, and maybe
the rain would go on like her—first touching her feet, rising to her
legs and her torso, making her wet and wetter until the clouds burst,
spilling all the water such that the sun and the moon would float
and shrink. And the world would turn into a sea with islands of their
bodies, holding onto each other with nowhere to go.

MILKY-EYED ORGASM SWALLOWS ME WHOLE

ONE NIGHT, WHILE ON the patio sofa touching myself, I call my orgasm, and maybe because of some curiosity on her part, she emerges and sits beside me, part sweat, part flesh. A ripple, stardust on her edges. Shimmering. A milky-eyed orgasm.

I joke that maybe I should introduce her to my parents—they don't have sex anymore. She laughs, places her delicate fingertips on my back, butterflies fluttering up my spine. "Let me ruin you." She speaks like a window opened in spring, her words touched by the pollen-beaded wind. Her teeth are small, pointed. Above us, a swollen yellow moon loiters.

"I was twelve when I first touched myself. By the time I felt you, you'd already left." I look at her in a questioning, assessing gaze.

"Your heart can only take so much of love," she explains. "I must protect you from yourself." The light around us grows frail. She inches towards me; her face looks blurry up close. "Everything is clearer after you are done with me," she whispers, tongues my ear. I feel butterflies rise up my spine.

My mother calls my name from somewhere inside the house. I conjure her up: thin lips reciting her love for stone-faced gods, little feet pacing the distance between her bedroom and the kitchen, the last time she was arguing with my father, their voices raised, insufferable. Their cold presence. How shameful it must be to endure a relationship without love or desire.

It's prayer time, I tell the orgasm. But she doesn't listen, her fingers are snug between my thighs, she is dirty-talking, words slipping out of her mouth strung in a thread of saliva. I bird-breathe, try to be as quick as I can.

The night shivers like a membrane.

My mother calls again. I hear her footsteps, imagine the disapproving look if she sees my unzipped shorts, my tank top strap below my shoulder, my left breast exposed. I try to push the orgasm away, but she doesn't leave. She is too happy to care, so she swallows me whole. My mother opens the patio door, her eyes averted in shame or disbelief, perhaps jealousy. The orgasm continues to work her magic, as if licking a wound deep inside me, sweet and slightly hurtful, tickling, biting all at once. "This is your living," she says, "this is your will, this is your prayer," until I come down like a wet bird.

"Stand up," my mother yells, her face beet red. "What's wrong with you?" She looks unbearably disgusted but wants to watch. Darkness spills around us.

I breathe in hard, feel the orgasm back in my bones, her pilot flame flickering satisfactorily between my legs.

"What's wrong with you?" my mother shouts again. Curses falling off her mouth like dry lumps of dirt.

I don't say anything, I keep listening, I keep looking up at the moon that cuts the night, a hot patch between us, my heat reflected off it like glaze.

PUNYA MITTI

A MAN IS TALKING in the corridor and my mother is hushing him to be quiet. I sit on the side of the bed and listen to the sound of digging. From the window, I see the head priest of our town squatting on the ground and Ma pouring the dug soil in his lap, the sky above the color of dirt. The monsoon has blown itself out, but like Ma says, rain comes like sadness, a splurge of water or a series of drops holding each other's hands before becoming one with the ground. The priest bows his head in gratitude before he walks to the end of the narrow road. Once away from our eyes, I know, he will sprinkle holy Gangajal on his body because he has been just outside a brothel, he has just begged a prostitute, my mother, for punya mitti to build the idol of goddess Durga for the upcoming festival.

"Babu," Haseena, my caretaker in Ma's absence, says, and runs her long fingers through my hair. She's wearing her favorite coral lipstick and salmon rouge, a round bindi between her bushy eyebrows. I bring my notebook, and Haseena checks the arithmetic homework she gave me yesterday. For quite some time, she has been my teacher, since no one would allow a prostitute's daughter in their school.

"When will I start school, Haseena?"

"Soon," she says, and marks the problems I must do again. "Let's play chess."

•

A sound like a loud clap wakes me up, neck-deep in darkness. Perhaps a lizard fell from the wall to the floor. Through the window, I see swarms of fireflies light up the jasmine vines, the bougainvillea covering the crevices of our old, condemned kotha, a house of a prostitute, the shame of society. During the day, it looks like any other house on the street. In another section of our home, a place I am not allowed to go, a celebration amplifies, and I hear Ma's voice singing, the tap of her ghunghroos. Men occasionally roar like firecrackers in the stream of her soulful ghazal. I get up and stand next to the window. The sky is a perfect square, like an ocean flecked with diamonds at night. Ma says the ocean churns and seethes, takes in all that is offered without attachment or aversion, and brings us rain. Her descriptions make me miss it even though I've never seen it. Closing my eyes, I imagine her hands carving elegant gestures, the chandelier on the ceiling carrying a million reflections of her charm.

When dawn comes bursting in my room, I am in the cave of my mother's body, her palm on my forehead, her curved toes next to my leg, lightly brushing even when she is snoring. Later in the morning, when I ask her to make Macher Jhol, she takes me to a spice and fish market, past the railway tracks, past the mills, far away from the courtyard and the little town I have known all my life.

"What is punya mitti, Ma?" I glance at her. She is wearing a peacock-blue sari and short sleeve blouse that best complements her walnut skin, crystal earrings dangling to her shoulders like a string of raindrops.

"Sacred soil," she says, pushing a hand against her sweaty forehead, then tucking a long stray hair to her tight, black bun.

"Is it true that goddess Durga's idol is made of punya mitti?"

"It's a part of goddess Durga, yes," my mother says with a frown, her perfectly arched eyebrows raised. I can see the heat is irritating her. Ahead, a crowd, gales of high-pitched voices of hawkers and sellers. Some men curiously glance at us—sly smiles and moving lips. Even though we are surrounded by noise, I can hear their lewd remarks hitting my ears as if I've stepped on a fire anthill. Ma tightens her grip around my wrist and rushes past the crowd toward the hawker who waves and calls her name.

After a brief bargaining war, Ma pulls out a wad of rupees from her blouse. She parts with it with great reluctance while I hold the fish in an old newspaper, our dinner, our treasure for the day.

In the kitchen attached to our bedroom, separate from rest of the house, Ma roasts the curry powder. I crush mustard seeds and cumin. Spices fry and pots boil. The room is veiled in steam, the tendrils licking my mother's forehead.

"If the soil in our yard is sacred, why do men condemn you?"

Ma shakes her head in dismissal. In the background, famous singer and thumri queen Begum Akhtar continues to croon.

"Once someone called you dirt, filth, a worm who needs to be burned and purified of her sins." The sound of my voice sad.

Ma looks at me.

"I heard it!"

"These men," she says, a flame of mockery in her explosive voice, "they curse me in the day, and they come to me at night. Drunk and hopeless, they swear on their children and confess their love for me. Then they joke with me asking if I could teach their wives how to satiate them, but I know they don't really want that. Any woman who knows, who is able to please herself and others, must be out of control, full of filth, dirt, and not worthy of matrimony."

A tear falls from the edge of her cheek and levels on the floor.

"It doesn't bother me that they call me whore, because I am loose and free."

I bring her a glass of water.

"Oh, about punya mitti." She gulps a mouthful, her neck slender in dim light, the movement of fluid behind her translucent skin. She stares at the ceiling for so long it makes me uncomfortable. "It is part clay collected from River Ganga's riverbanks, part cow's urine, part soil from nishiddho palli like this brothel. The earth from a forbidden territory is most sacred because those who visit our world leave behind their virtues at the doorstep." Then she pauses, as if preparing an argument to challenge an invisible opponent. "It's just another idea to feed the ego of men."

I don't understand all of what she said, but I can see the pain moving in my mother's body, glowing as it spreads across her limbs and her torso, the skin surging with pink, bright orange hues. I hold her hand. It's warm, still pulsing with hurt.

"What happened to me, Babu, I won't let it happen to you," she says, fierce against my ear.

The following evening, when it's time for Ma to leave for the dance court, I watch her touch her makeup, the rose blooming in her cheeks, a light sparkle on her forehead and next to the inner edge of her eyes, the circles below them darker. She brushes her lips on my forehead and I know I won't remove the mark of her mouth until I bathe the next day.

Later, I sob in Haseena's lap. "I made Ma cry."

"Your Ma is tough," Haseena says. Her deft fingers rake my scalp. "She's Durga."

•

Next fall, I get admission in a school in a nearby town, Haseena is to accompany me. They pack my notebooks, my school uniform, my slippers, and the chessboard.

The night before, Ma and I sit on the stairs in the patio, the sky swathed in night-chilled ribbons of purple.

"I'll miss your Macher Jhol, Durga Ashtami," I say and place my palm in hers. "I'll miss waiting for you, sitting outside with you."

"Do you want to see something, Babu?" she asks, her eyes tired but sparkling.

We take a walk around the kotha, onto the road, across the fields, into a small place where half-finished Durga idols sit. Some with blank faces, some only a body—round, smooth-muscled, cream-toned. Others have etched eyes, fish-tailed, kohl-lined, their brightness about to spill. I watch my mother standing next to a full-size statue, her fingers tapping on the hardened clay as if it's her own skin, her gaze liquid in reverence, a tender staccato conversation of the body and the divine, the breathless silence between them.

•

In summers when the school is out, Haseena is away visiting her folks and I stay with Ma. She paints my nails, I color her eyes smoky, the crow's feet prominent, the wrinkles in her neck like slim pleats in her sari. We watch the swirling fan in her room, the curtains swaying to the monsoon poems we sing. Our thigh muscles quiver, dancing from a low squat, sweat beading on our foreheads and upper lips. Ma spins me stories of faraway villages, cycles of seasons, famines and floods, the forests and wild animals bursting at the edge of settlements where men and women always kept a machete and hardly slept. The sunset eyes of a man-eater Bengal tiger, the tall plants crushed under a herd of wild elephants, now and then an inky ejaculation from a red octopus in secret passageways of a river, upturned turtles, the insatiable swamps that blobbed as they sank and suffocated fishermen alive. I've witnessed it all, she'd say—the demon who entered a young girl's body and caused uproar in the village, a witch was summoned from Banaras—she danced all night, spun and leapt in the air with bulging eyes, skulls around her neck. The next morning the girl was cured; she was free of the dirt that plagued her. More stories, I'd say and close my eyes. Years later, Haseena admits that the girl was my mother, and the demon was a middle-aged leader of her village who spoiled her. To avoid shame, her parents sold her to a prostitute in another town. Since then, Ma dreamt of a witch who cured her. Until I was born, and she found a purpose to raise me, to love me.

On Ma's right arm, I see a bruise, small, perhaps a nail mark, but bright. Maybe someone had hurt her, maybe it's a mark of love. I am eighteen, she is forty, there are rooms in her heart I don't wander into. Out of respect, out of love, out of avoiding hurt or staying ignorant. It feels safe to not know the men and women she endures, to not talk about this boy I kissed—his mouth warm and hungry, his legs pressed against my thigh, his hardness eager to plant inside my soil. It feels sanctified to stay in our cocoon of mother and daughter and sense the grooves next to our mouths deepen when we see each other and smile. The rest of the world melts away as I rest my head on her beating heart. It's smooth like the surface of a lake, rippling with light. I run my fingers over her bruise as if my recurring touch will heal it.

•

I am hundreds of miles away in a college in Kolkata when Ma suffers cardiac arrest or a stroke. Possibly she was unable to bear the distance between us for so long. No one knows. By the time I arrive, she is cremated where unclaimed corpses are burned. Haseena collects her ashes for me to disperse in the river, to relieve her from this world.

Inside Ma's room, I hold the earthen pot in my hand, my fingers slippery with humidity, my eyes hot, angry with tears, searching for any sign of her in the golden-brown remains. We've spent so much time together and yet, at this moment, all the unsaid questions rush like blood in my head—about desire, about belonging and body. About loneliness. It seems impossible to breathe here, now, without her.

"Has the priest come in to ask for punya mitti for this year's Durga puja?" I ask, my voice an echo in her room filled with too many memories, a blur of Ma's presence next to the window.

"Any day now, Babu," Haseena says, and presses her lips against my forehead, soft plumpness touching my sorrow. Now she is everything I have, to navigate the past, to mourn about my mother.

In the front yard, I dig the earth with my bare hands. When the priest arrives, I fill his lap with wet lumps sprinkled with a fine dust, the sunlight reflected from them like a hundred flames from earthen lamps floating in water. The air goes still as if the entire attention of the world has descended into this small, forbidden yard of my mother's kotha. The hairs on my arms rise as I imagine skilled hands of artisans shaping the clay—the best Durga idol they've built so far, immaculate. As thousands of devotees bow to the kilowatt gaze of the goddess, and at the end of the festival carry her on their shoulders, bid goodbye to my ingrained Ma in the River Hooghly as she floats until she's submerged. As I hold my palms together in a prayer, long after the priest has left. As rich, dark pads of punya mitti stick on my hands—their fragrance outing all other thoughts, their closeness, their tenderness like a heart muscle torn and sewn with ache.

SAANWALEE

MY MOTHER MADE ME SLEEP in moonlight to improve my dark complexion. She laid out a folding bed, tied the ends of a mosquito net to the four columns on the patio and instructed me to pull the blanket only when it got unbearably cold.

"Allow the light to get absorbed, to make you fairer," she instructed.

I fell asleep to the bright button of the moon rising and falling, its dye whitewashing the world and filling my nose with mucus. In the mornings, my mother inspected my skin, a grim resignation in her eyes. During the bath hour, she rubbed my body with a paste of wheat fiber mixed with honey and sandalwood. My limbs and torso rippled like a sea floor with bumps. Red and blue. Bruises, cuts bright and raw, eventually swallowed by a darker, healing layer. "No one likes a saanwalee girl," my mother hissed, "no one," and scrubbed harder every subsequent time.

"But what about Munir who follows me after school all the way home?"

"Munir isn't yours, he's engaged to your cousin Razia," she yelled, and emptied a bucket full of water on my head.

On certain licoricey nights, I imagined Munir walking behind me, his hands in his pocket, a light bulge growing between his legs, igniting a dark inside me, between the synchronized pulses of my heart. I felt one with the night as I touched myself thinking of his sparse, brown beard tickling my torso as he ate my tanned pigments and foamed them out of his mouth, a pale liquid skin.

•

My mother liked to wear powder-pink and sky-blue salwar suits that went well with her pale complexion. She met my dark-skinned father on a bus. Their families knew each other, often met at the masjid. My parents were a combination like steeped tea and milk. Whenever my father called me, I said, Abbu, with a ring of affection. Everyone loved Abbu.

"Don't cry," he said and ran his fingers in my hair, when my mother was unbearable. Then he'd share a joke and we would start laughing like nothing happened. I told him, one day I'll marry a handsome man like him. We'll live in a mansion and own cars. This handsome man and I will love each other forever. At first, Abbu nodded his head, then he laughed so hard his eyes watered, he coughed, and his face turned red, alien, and primitive, like a creepy Muppet.

•

The monsoon started, and I started sleeping in my room. Strings of raindrops on the windows, on the trees, flowers bowed under the weight of water. The quick, creeping dullness of the evening slipping into a wet, warm dark. During these nights, I woke up multiple times. What had roused me from sleep, I don't know. The slap of water on the roof before it dripped into the ground, a truck horn, the sound of crickets and frogs, whatever nameless shadow drew me from dreams into the waking black. I moved my finger in the inky air. It was like me—swift, smooth, a spirit enveloped in a shadow, a tight, thickened bud. I wanted to step into my mother's bedroom and show her I was the night, and no matter the effort and time, she could not change the color of the night. Come morning, the world reassembled, and my mother handed me a paste of turmeric and milk, the mix cool on my forehead, on my chin. Under a rare day flecked with sunbeams and not lightning, my skin glowed like molten chocolate. After a month, not seeing any improvement, my mother gritted her teeth and cursed the light that reflected my skin like a solid, rebellious, sooty pigment. I placed hands over my ears.

I napped after school and listened to the radio at midnight, watching the square of sky from my window turning dark and darker, lighter at the edges as if a TV screen switched off. I dreamt of traveling alone to wormholes of different continents and meeting men, feeling their breath and heartbeat, with a light around their faces as they leaned in to kiss me.

·

In our ancestral two-storied home, I found Razia sitting at the dressing table, gazing into the circular mirror that leaned against the wall. Her bangs curled, her cheeks, her neck glossy, pale like plastic Barbie's.

"Will you take some pictures for me?" Razia handed her phone to me. "Just what you see in the mirror," she instructed.

After I finished, Razia pulled the muslin over the mirror. "The cloth protects the beauty of my reflection," she said.

"From whom?"

"Dead spirits and jealous girls," she replied, a sly smile escaping from the corner of her mouth.

I shrugged and picked up a box of Jolen creme bleach from the dresser.

"You can have it," Razia said as she cropped what seemed like the edges of my dark fingers from the photos. I turned my gaze away.

Of course, Razia was not always like this. She was a loudmouth know-it-all fair-skinned girl. Only two years older than me, she had always been winning a one-sided competition of being beautiful and likeable. I had been good at school, mostly obedient and respectful to my parents and teachers. Slowly, though, a rift had formed and expanded. And now, with her engagement to Munir, she had achieved something I was told I never would.

Outside the window, a wasp's nest hung like a lantern suspended from long pole. I wondered if there were wasps inside it right now, listening to our conversation. If they understood human sounds, if the darker-colored wasps were treated any differently from the lighter ones. I stared at the gray wattle, its thin paper-like structure that moved in the air as if about to break but didn't.

•

I wore low-cut blouses, short skirts. I smiled at Munir. Sunlight fell on my skin, coppering the curves of my body. The days of sleeping in moonlight and DIY masks were long gone. All my mother did now was consult a local matchmaker who called her every Saturday, and together they deliberated connections in the family, salaries of her possible son-in-law, saanwalaa in skin but golden at heart.

Optimistic, I followed the instructions to bleach my skin as if it were the solution to my life's problems in a gray square box. I let it sit, fume my temples and nose, a thousand needles plucking my dark. Then with a soft butter knife I scraped the white paste and emerged bronze.

•

One day after class, Munir and I walked to an abandoned train car. The old railway station was a kilometer away from my home, a secret place tucked between a grove of banyans and gulmohars. "Teedt, teedt," the birds cried in unison from the transmission lines from which they had taken flight. Inside the car, Munir unbuttoned my blouse, ran his fingers over my arms. I looked past his lush hair, past the square window, the old platform, the city's name graffitied, unrecognizable, a gnarly tree next to the tin-roofed restrooms. He sucked my mouth and the little veins on his forehead pulsed, the grotesque, cobwebbed ceiling above us like a veiled belly. Cut off from the world, isolated in time and space in a train compartment, who was to say what belonged to me—Munir's mouth, my luminous skin color, a setting sun, the shady place we were in, I could never tell anyone. I wondered if my hunger was saanwalee too: a shimmering dark tunnel. In the distance, a train whistled, the vibration approaching. I cupped my palms over his ears so all he could hear were our moans boomeranging off the walls of the coach, all we were—mirrors protecting the reflection of each other's bodies, our mouths open to swallow whatever we could sink our teeth into.

•

The day Munir and Razia got married, I danced the night away with Munir's friend, Asim. He brought ice cream, coke mixed with vodka. The music was loud, everybody letting go. "Sweetheart," he said, and led me away from the dance floor. Watching us leave, Munir shifted uncomfortably at the celebratory table, while Razia waved, threw kisses at us. Behind the bushes, we set the glasses and the night, threaded each other's words in our saliva. Asim pulled up my ghaghra, dug my hole and made it a river. The air became slicker, the crickets stiller. He pressed his nails on my back, bit my nipples, little drops of blood pooling, settling. It felt better than when my mother scrubbed my skin in hope of something it could never be. I pictured her walking in the party with a bowl of dessert and an untouched spoon, looking for me to introduce to dark-skinned bachelor boys, words scrambling on her lips, "Have you seen my daughter?"

In the distance, silhouettes of people drifted guffawing, cursing about their relationship problems, their suits and jewelry holding onto their bodies, feeling the pressure of their breath and expectations to look special. A helicopter hovered, its Christmasy lights licked by the night. The moonlight peaked and fell over my naked body, glowed it like whipped coffee.

"You look exotic," Asim said, his tongue a leech on my sweaty neck, a gust of warmth from his mouth mixed with the October crisp.

"IknowIknowIknow," I said, and held his light-skinned face. In the tinted blue air, it didn't look much different from mine, his eyes the darkest center pulling me in, never to escape.

I bit his lip. He let out a sharp scream. "Sorry," I whispered, "shh, shh," and kept licking it, nibbling it, until it no longer bled, until it matched the night's shade.

MY MOTHER VISITS ME IN AMERICA
AND IS OFFENDED BY WHAT
THE DISHWASHER CAN DO

SHE ASKS IF THERE'S a human inside who scrubs the dishes and puts them back as they came in. I laugh, kiss her on her forehead, dipping my nose into her thinning hair.

I smear creamy lotion on my mother's callused palms. White settles in the trench of her life line. Years of washing dishes for restaurants to send me to school, to buy books and uniforms after Pa died. Her back curved on dhobi ghats wringing out towels, sheets, her long face against the fabric on the clothesline, siphoning damp relief. Now, next to the sink where she has rinsed her life, a dishwasher is draining erasure into the creases on her forehead. During the day, she sticks her finger in the tufts of silverware holders, presses the soap pellets on her wash-annulled palms, their scent embroidered into her shadow. After dinner, her rosary-shaped eyes wait until the red LED of the machine turns off, expecting someone to walk out drenched in water, laced in froth.

"I haven't embraced the porcelain in days," she complains, her eyes dull with boredom. "My limbs are sore from underuse."

"Ma, I have it all so you can rest now!" I plunge my gloved hands into the greasy dishwater in the sink, a mechanical whirring of the motor starting in the background.

"I wake up at nights," my mother says, "and grow sad about the world. It's dying because there's too much smartness and not enough touch."

I shake my head and hear the mushy hurt of her guts—deep breaths, snotted air, a washcloth-cringed wetness split between us.

"It's a curse not to use your gift to serve. Besides, what do you do your entire life if not clean? First, the skin for good health, then the tongue with silence, and last, the mind with compassion," my mother says.

I don't know what to say, so I interlace my fingers in hers. They don't fit as they once did. There are gaps from which the light escapes.

LAWNS

SINCE HIS WIFE LEFT HIM, my neighbor, a scientist, mows his lawn at midnight. The noise makes my head throb. One night, I walk up to his house. He stops the mower, sits on the front steps. Self-loathing teems from him. I pause before I walk back. I hear him cry.

•

There is a bird on my patio, struggling to stand. It makes me think of the scientist, his head bent over manuals in his lab, his neck sore when he straightens. Later in the day, from my second-floor bedroom, I watch him by the pool. At this hour, the light leans its back against the slanted roof. I go around his yard. White plastic bags from the supermarket, bottles of wine on his patio. I sit with him. He looks at me, some sort of awareness and embarrassment in his eyes and a brief flare of anger. *I should have done something to stop her,* he says. I hold his hand. The water ripples our silhouettes. A lone cloud in the sky splits the sun.

•

I stop by the scientist's home again after a night of drinking. He opens the door, his hair disheveled as if he has just walked out of his lab after several failed experiments. When I kiss him, he hesitates for a moment, then kisses back, leads me to a guest room. He says the bedroom is reserved for his wife. Later, drunk and roped in cigarette smoke, he claims his wife's stuff takes up all the space in his house. We dig a large hole next to the pool, bury her name and her belongings.

•

From my upstairs room, I can see the mound of dirt in the scientist's backyard. A shoot of grass on it. I avoid meeting him as if coming to terms with a loss. He leaves messages on my phone: *When will I see you?* My mailbox looks like a dragon with red, yellow, paper wings taped to it, calling my name, the letters from *I need you* curling like distilled compounds in a chemical reaction. His misery ruffles in the cicada-clogged air, shimmering blue if looked on intently.

•

The next time I'm with him, he asks how I coped after my husband left me for another woman. I pull the sheets up to my chin. He flicks the edges of my hair, his toes wiggle on my legs. *Your ceiling needs another coat of paint,* I say, the words weighing down the edges of my lips. The afternoon sun oils our bodies. We shower together, his big hand rubbing soap on my shoulders, washing the foam like a discarded memory. Later, at night, from my second-floor bedroom, I see him digging in his backyard, pulling out pieces of clothing, smelling them, holding them close.

For hours, I sit on the edge of my bed. I remember the night my husband left, I fell through emptiness. Void became our parting song. I want to believe there's more to this life than loving and losing. There's more than just longing.

•

The scientist's house is dark. The night is pure with no stars. The mower is outside his garage. I turn it on, go around his house several times, until the machine sputters turning the grass to ground, until the space around me is iridescent green. Until he's out, sitting on the steps, watching, as if saying, *If we don't ache for those who've left us, what then can we give?*

NARTAKI

THERE CAME A TIME when the eldest girl of the six kids living in an old house on the hill could bear the caregiving duties no longer and fled her home. She left carrying only the clothes on her back. After traveling for days and begging for food, she came to a settlement of tribal dancers who lived in tents, lit by earthen lamps, crows lined around the perimeter. The girl asked for shelter and was brought in front of the caretaker everyone called Mother.

"This is not a refuge for a girl who ran away from home," Mother said, her upper lip twitching.

"Everyone in my family is dead," the girl said, her eyes so bright, as if with fever.

"Very well," Mother said, and picked up a round mirror in the dip of her long skirt. The girl felt her sharp gaze on her back as she walked away from Mother's luxurious tent into an ordinary one with an old cot and a rusted trunk to keep her few things.

•

Mother was relentlessly lazy and surrounded by beautiful, sly women deft at dancing and singing, at making their thoughts her own. She spent the day in her tent, lounging on a plush mattress, her feet underneath her hips, her large body looking like a twisted knot. The girl served Mother strictly to the letter—every dawn she walked two kilometers to get freshly squeezed cow milk, washed her clothes, starched, and ironed them, applied buffalo curd on her puffy, blotchy face, and gave her a luxuriating sandalwood bath. The work led her from task to task as though a finger slipping through the rosary. In the evenings, the girl lingered around the dancers getting ready—rubbing a chalk of color on their lips, pink, fluorescent dust on their cheeks, tapping their wrists and necks with perfumes from bulbed bottles, wearing lehengas and covering their faces with bright, transparent veils before stepping on the stage. Earnestly, the girl watched them dancing with a column of earthen pots on their heads or landing straight on a steel plate after somersaulting in the air. Later the dancers would return to their tents, their mouths leaned into each other's ears, wreathed in murmurs about the men who whistled at them. Alone in her tent, the girl stared at the ceiling and thought of her family, her mother's anger uppermost in her mind, if one of them wandered this far looking for her. Somehow being invisible in the settlement soothed her for the time being. She fell asleep dreaming as one of the dancers—a small flask balanced on her forehead as she whirled and twirled, once so fast she woke up. It was then she decided to practice on her way to get the milk—standing upright on grazing buffaloes and donkeys—her first step toward balance. *Mind before body,* she kept chanting, like she'd heard the performers when they practiced. In a few months she could tiptoe on the feeding animals—crawl in narrow ditches and jump from the cliff into the river, let the gushing water bend and twist her like an octopus.

When she performed for the first time in front of Mother, everyone marveled at the girl's grace as long as she lip-synced to Mother's sweet voice, since her own was coarse. The girl, beaming with joy, realized no other part of her life had mattered, all of it had been gathering pace toward this moment.

Soon the girl established herself as the nartaki, the main dancer. The knowledge of what had to be done steadied her feet and arms— she performed blindfolded, throwing small, sharp knives at the audience without injuring anyone. Some of the dancers warned Mother of the growing popularity of the girl with the audience, her friendship with powerful men from the ruling parties in the adjoining cities who regularly came to watch her. Afraid to lose her influence, Mother invited the girl into her tent, offering her koel's blood as a means to sweeten her voice, the girl's portion mixed with venom from a deadly scorpion.

As the girl drank the dank, pungent blood, something snatched her outside of her body. When she returned to herself, the reflection in the mirror showed her awash in blood, her right pinky shaped like a stinger and Mother's body open like a split pomegranate. When she stepped outside Mother's tent, she felt she had walked out of a womb, covered in Mother's fat and gore, her sight gleaming with the wonder of a newborn. Some women shrieked, some stood in silent disbelief, their collective foreheads covered in a hazy terror. She asked one of them to transfer her belongings into Mother's tent and realized how hypnotizing she sounded. When some women suggested they cremate Mother, some talked about a burial, the girl-bird suggested to feed it to the crows, and all the women brought their knives and swords, smiling and chopping away, as if nothing happened.

The girl-bird massaged her teeth with cloves, applied powdered snakeskin on her eyelids like Mother used to. Once a month—a frequency determined by trial and error to keep her voice melodious—she drank koel's blood tinged with scorpion's venom, and to avoid killing anyone, she chained herself to the strong bedposts until she returned to herself, her hair disheveled, her eyes crimson-flecked. Koel's blood made her skin shine like a mirror. When she sang, her voice rose above everything—the stage, the streetlights, a perfect pitch, translucent without a rupture, like it belonged not only to humans but everything breathing around her. When she danced, the cows and dogs herded, the snakes spiraled, the birds flew in a circular pattern, the men, women, and children swayed as if in a trance, their eyes mesmerized to a splendor of colors and cadence.

It went on until the girl-bird fell in love with a local municipal officer who used to visit during her performances. She didn't care that he had a paunch and his eyes dropped to his chin. She didn't care he was married with two older boys age appropriate to be her suitors. He was the only one who seemed unfazed by her voice. During the day they smoked pot, got on his motorbike. They drove across the fields and the long winding roads, through the city, as fast as they could. "My queen," the officer slurred at her, then kissed her fingers and arms, elbows, his left hand grabbing her thigh through her skirt. She twisted and twitched in arousal. Intoxicated, their bodies wilted into incomplete sex until the girl-bird woke up to mosquitoes buzzing in her ears, a lurking moon behind a cloud like a shy bride.

When the officer's wife came to know of her husband's indiscretions, she threw him out of their house and cursed the girl-bird to die from the sweetness in her voice. Homeless, the officer started living in the settlement. Together, he and the girl-bird drank and slept until late. The performers considered it a bad omen, a man cursed by his wife living amongst them, and advised the girl-bird against it. Sagged under liquor and love, she laughed it off and grew reckless with feeding the crows and disciplining the dancers, canceling her performances. Gradually the crowds shrank and most of the women left to look for other settlements. Once the neglect took over, it was forever.

In the absence of koel's blood, the sound in the girl-bird's throat crystallized into sharp lumps of sugar, her neck swollen, ruptured, unable to turn, move. It was only when she couldn't speak that she realized the municipal officer was deaf—he made out the words by watching her lip movements and therefore was not under her spell. Lying on an old cot in her tent holed in the wind and rain, she knew he had left; it had been days since she had seen him. She could feel the space around her tighten under the force of loneliness and loss. Syrupy tears glaciered on her cheeks. Attracted to the sweetness, the ants darkened her face, their antennae and legs stuck in the viscous fluid, their bodies mounting on top of each other. The sound that had been staggering in her body came out like a fatigued song and her warm mouth opened, an orifice for the ants to sink as if in quicksand.

Eyes closed, she imagined a soft remembrance of her house on the hill, until the front door flung open and a heap of tattered possessions with no familiar sounds of her parents or siblings unfolded before her. A shadow like Mother's slipped across the window. Giant crows flew around under a ceiling of dim lights, their young ones shrieking from the attic, koels with wrung necks sprawled on the living room floor, rotted beyond recognition.

MOTHER, PREY

THE GIRL WAS TEN when she discovered she had a womb. It bloomed red. The same year, she learned about space. Booster rockets to escape gravity, separated and lost forever. Her mother bagged items in a grocery store, *Mary*, an embroidered badge pinned on her dress. She ate leftovers, said "Thank you," and smiled even in her sleep. The girl caught bugs, filled her mouth with dirt, tasted the salt and spit. Passing through the hallway on her way out, she tipped her head in the direction of the statue of Lord Ganesha her mother got on her trip to India while she was still married to the girl's father. The Elephant God fascinated the girl with his ever-compassionate eyes, his large body positioned comfortably over a small rat.

Her mother kept the girl's milk teeth in a velvet pouch. They looked like eggs of a small bird. When the girl got braces, the metal dug into her gums. It hurt to smile but she thought at least it was genuine.

•

The girl practiced falling at fifteen. First a two-foot platform, then a building, finally a plane. Moments before the parachute opened, green and brown squares hazed below, eyepatches of clouds. Her mother refused to sign consent forms, tried to stop her but finally allowed her and posted her pictures on her Facebook page, shared

on her WhatsApp. Adventurous which her mother spelled *avinturus.*
She mentioned the girl tried falling from her womb feet first.

●

At sixteen. The girl became gluten-free and started swimming. Her
mother said, "Everyone has limited breaths, don't waste them under-
water."

While watching the Discovery Channel, the girl learned that
humpbacks spend their winters in warm waters. Mothers with newborn calves travel thousands of miles to feast on krill. Their haunting
calls carry for miles beneath the sea. Listening to them, she wondered
if they were ever loved enough.

Every night, the girl kissed her mother's papery cheeks, felt her
petite ribs when she kneaded her arms through her mother's blouse.
Sweat and tension, a day materialized. A whining noise from her
mother's mouth when she checked the pantry, her bank account. *I
don't want to grow as fearful and anxious as you,* the girl thought as she
pressed her chest against her mother's.

Ways to escape ownership, the girl googled. Hysterectomy showed
up.

●

During her summer break, the girl started visiting bars with her
friends. She met men with deep voices and long, biblical names. They
smelled of dismembered deer, gutted fish. Sometimes they pushed
her in the corner, held her face in their large hands rough from split-
ting rocks and cutting trees, as if inspecting if she was appropriate to
be fucked. At home, her mother shouted at her, told her she should
stop being a dumb cunt. They argued in the kitchen over the girl's
short dresses and her hairstyles, the outdoors and the indoors, the
men she continued to see. And the girl believed her mother never

wanted to be a mother in the first place. Or maybe a part of her did.

When school started, the girl pulled out her father's old sweaters from her mother's trunk. They smelled of mothballs. Their interlocking diamond and cable patterns. One with a cowl neck felt like armor around her. When she slept, she dreamt of the faces of older men from the bars looking into two holes in her face that used to be her eyes.

•

After her mother died, the girl, now a woman, saw a therapist. Told him about her mother's slow-mouthed songs in her nightmares: her voice separated from her buried body, sobs, whispers through an open vent. She started watching movies about repressed memories, dreams and fantasies, signs and symbols uncovering the hidden origins of one's existence, of inheriting one's mother's fears.

"A life starts with a burial," the woman's mother murmured in her dreams. "The only way to love is to either birth something or to destroy it." The woman performed headstands to spill her memories, refused to lie on her back because it reminded her of her mother lying in the casket.

•

The woman was in her thirties when she fell in love with a college professor. He let her believe that she was finally connecting the dots, experiencing the world as it is. Attraction to him felt vast and inescapable. He had half a couch, half a house in the country from his first marriage. His daughter was teased at school because she was blind in one eye. The woman promised to bring in the other half.

Lace and tulle, cheap wine at the wedding. She brought fresh bread to her mouth but couldn't eat. Her belly showed, its gluten-free walls grimed from expanding. No parachute between her legs to hold if the baby decided to come headfirst, only stories to crown him. Her breasts milked an ocean. She could hear the whales calling out to their calves who were now mothers themselves. During her delivery, the woman held her mother's nametag, folded her body like paper. Her baby dropped full, his shallow, white breathing wooled her heart. "Mothermothermother," he sang and dug his uneven nails on her skin. Marked her as his prey.

A DULL, SILVER ARC OF LIVING

My husband and I are parked on the edge of a lake, eating Subway sandwiches. We're returning from a wedding in a neighboring city.

"It's Karwa Chauth tomorrow," I say, passing the water bottle to him, the moonlight laminating our windshield.

"I'll be fasting for you," he says, lettuce and cheese in his teeth.

"Why?"

"Six months ago, when you were hospitalized and no meds could reduce your fever for several days, I made a vow. You started showing improvement after that evening. Also, I won't be the first man to fast—"

"Until this time tomorrow," I say, "after the moon comes up."

He doubles back on my sentence. In this light, his eyes squint as if taking aim, his face grows tense. Outside, the surface of water glimmers. My husband has an air of mystery around him and that's what I love about him, but it's a long, grueling old Hindu tradition.

"It's too hard, you don't have to—"

He puts his hand around me. "This is for your long and healthy life. Not finishing it will have serious consequences for you." His voice strangely deeper, fuller.

"Don't be silly—" I kiss the crack on his chin from a childhood accident falling off the bike.

"Well, did you ever break it when you used to fast for me?" His eyebrows are raised, his forehead creased. The question hangs in the middle of the whiff of his aftershave and the warmth of our breaths tickling my nose. I move my face away and sneeze.

•

At this hour before daybreak, our bedroom looks like a view into a small spaceship. I kiss my husband on his ear when the alarm goes off. "Go back to sleep. I will go eat some sargi and drink water now," he whispers and closes the bedroom door softly after him.

•

From the window, the darkness fades around the horizon. A violet dawn is immersed in stars.

I stretch under the sheets. No water and food for him after the sun comes up. Until moonrise. Since my childhood, my mother had been conferring upon me the rituals, the shlokas of how a married woman should be devoted to her husband. I had seen her perform the ceremony of Karwa Chauth for my father—henna on palms and feet, painted nails. Decorating the pooja ghar with flowers and rango-li and waiting for the moonrise in a starlit sky. In the first year of my marriage, my mother-in-law offered me sargi on the dawn of Karwa Chauth. A glass of sweetened, hot milk with seviyan. Observing this fast as per our scriptures brought sons and prosperity, cured illness, she said. Breaking it without seeing the moon would bring ill fate to the family, especially the spouse. Then she dabbed some sindoor along the parting line of my hair, wishing me a life of togetherness and a meaningful death as a married woman. By evening, I could hardly walk, dizzy with hunger but mostly thirst. When the moon rose, my husband stood tall—his breath fragrant with a mouth-fresh-ening mix of coconut flakes and fennel seeds—and handed me a glass of water, my first sip in twenty hours.

"Was it all that difficult?" He grinned with childlike innocence.

•

When I get out of the bathroom, my husband is pacing in the bedroom, his right hand circling his stomach.

If I offered him food or water, he'd dismiss it, saying I don't think he's strong enough to finish the fast. "Hunger is an illusion," I say. "You can do it."

"I know, I know," he says, irritated. The angle of the light on his face makes him look thinner.

•

My husband eyes two aloo parathas with mango pickle, a cup of cardamom-ginger chai I've made for myself. He licks his chapped lips.

"Do you remember the time when I told you I dreamt of parathas on the days I fasted?" I ask.

His eyes are focused on my plate. I become conscious of the way I chew the buttered bread, imbibe the sweet tea.

•

The sun is falling west. My husband decides to take a nap.

I run my hand through his hair. Shiny black locks. Deep brown forehead. They say even between what we touch, there's an atomic gap, a gap that can never be overcome.

"This isn't as easy as it seems," he confesses.

I want to say, *It's only a myth, no harm done if you break it now.* But I keep massaging his scalp with my fingertips. The room sinks into a deeper silence.

•

My husband looks frail as he pulls out a chair. His elbows rest on the dining table, his palms cup around an imaginary mug while I boil milk and water, stir instant coffee with sugar. The chair creaks as he leans forward. I inch the cup toward him.

"No," he says, and gets up, hunched as if hurt by the air alone.

•

In the evening, we watch a South Asian channel playing Karwa Chauth songs, songs of devotion and love, unbreakable loyalty. Then he showers and wears a white churidar and a long red kurta, the golden chain around his neck a gift from my mother at our wedding.

As night approaches, he prepares his thali to worship the moon. Flowers, a pinch of vermillion and turmeric, a few rice grains, while I order takeout from an Indian restaurant—aloo gobi curry, dal makhani, achari baingan with tandoori rotis. He chants how Lord Shiva fasted for an indefinite time when Gauri, his wife, fell ill and there was no hope of her recovery. With his continuous fasting and reverence for his spouse, Shiva brought Gauri back to life and since then, they've been eternal partners.

•

We drive to the outskirts of the city where there are no buildings obstructing the sky to see if the moon has risen. October is in full bloom, crisp air, fallen leaves, frost slowly taking hold. Bunnies scurry in and out of nearby bushes. We sit in a deserted parking lot of an old industrial area. My husband is unable to stay still in his seat, his fingers fret.

"Do you want me to be your spouse again? In your next life?"

"Yes," he says, and rubs his palms together and breathes into them. "It's more fun to be with you than being alone, even when we're just watching TV, or working in our offices, or talking to someone else on the phone."

"That could be anyone instead of me."

"Could be," he pauses, "but I want it to be you. I don't know—it's like playing the same game over and again. The only thing left to do is to do it better."

We exchange our slippers, he wears my bangle, I put on his watch. It feels like a wedding ceremony. From the windshield, the stars look as if sewn flat against the sky, waiting to be undone. Then they slowly disappear.

•

The next morning when I wake up, my head is on the steering wheel, his seat pushed back as far as it can go, his mouth open. He wakes up with a jolt.

"Did the moon—"

"I don't know," I say. The sky is glittering with a light so bright, it's hard to look at it. "Let's go home."

"No, the moon has to be here, faint by now, but here," he insists. "I can do it," he whispers. I press my lips on his forehead. "Please let's stay for some more time," he begs. Something inside me is seized by his devotion, his belief that he might fail himself if he doesn't go through the entire fast. Sometimes being offered a complete submission to a notion feels like the very evidence that you've been a fake.

•

Another night slips in, and then another. I check the news with the little charge remaining in my phone. There are no reports of the moon missing. It's been a few days. My husband can hardly move. In the back of the car, I find a black satin eye mask, an old catalog from Ethan Allen, an opened bag of chips. A packed sandwich from our trip. An electric candle. When I take out a handful of chips for him, he looks at me and mouths, *I can do it. Promise me we won't leave until we see the moon.* His breath is dry, foul, his teeth a fence. He sleeps most of the time, his head rubbing hard on the seat that is hoarding some of his hair. He's ripping out like a stitch. Provoked by my own hunger, I pick a few chips and stop—all those years, did I fast for his long life like a dutiful wife, or was I just waiting for the hours to pass, pretending to be devoted to him? Until tired of feeling excessively hungry and inadequate on Karwa Chauth days, I stopped following the tradition. My husband said he didn't mind, and I luxuriated in the newfound absence of rituals and beliefs I thought were blind faith.

I glance at the chips, slip them back into the bag. Inside the car, my husband's eyes are barely open. I kiss them and want to cry. I want to pull him up, shake him with love and anger, *Look at you! Why are you doing this? Please, I'm begging you, let's go home.*

I want to say, *I'll do anything, if it means you'll live.*

•

While he's dozing, I walk toward a grove a few yards away from us. I turn on the electric candle and place it in between the farthest branches of two intertwined trees I can reach.

"The moon has risen," I shout several times as I run back to the vehicle, unsure how long the candle's battery will last.

He rubs his eyes, looking in my direction.

"There." I point to the candle in the midst of the branches, barely luminous.

He folds his hands in prayer. His eyes are sunken deep in their sockets, he's hardly awake. I put a water bottle to his mouth, swallowing a chunk of air, relieved. He takes a few sips drooling a stream from the corner of his mouth. Then he closes his eyes again. It's getting chilly and I shiver with the excitement of returning home as I buckle his seatbelt. My body feels stiff and thin. The edges of my arms blur in the darkening air. My husband giggles in his sleep and then the sullen hum of the car fills the silence. I'm cautious as I drive back, my fingers going numb from no exercise and restricted movements.

•

Our driveway is littered with newspapers, the mailbox overflowing with envelopes and packages. Our lawn is a lively mess of the wildflowers we'd been trying to protect it from.

"It will take forever to go through this," my husband says in his drowsy voice, his face slackened into seriousness, his left hand rubbing a circle on my thigh as I cross an ocean of junk, the tires squealing and crushing pieces of our life.

•

Inside, the house is stinking so badly I can hardly breathe. Rotting produce and cubes of decayed time. My husband pulls out the leftovers from the fridge and starts stuffing the chunks of potatoes in his mouth, the tomato curry staining his lips. He licks the empty Styrofoam boxes and aluminum foil.

•

Under the fluorescent light in the kitchen, my skin looks transparent—my muscles visible, split, the peeping bones—disappearing, atom by atom, as if self-destructing on a quiet timer. My husband drops his food and comes close, his wide-set eyes staring, his mouth opened in a shriek I can hardly hear. I try to focus but all I see is the blurry outline of his head, his shoulders, his weak arms dragging me to our bedroom, his tears soaking my skin. My nerves fire on and off, and something pulls the air out of my lungs, my eyes lidless, drying. My husband's touch feels closer than ever, as if it's mine. His lips are on my mouth or what's left of it, and I can taste the food that's a part of him with my disappearing tongue, my teeth, my hunger I held back on the days I fasted, a sensation so terrifyingly freeing and fulfilling.

From the window, the Big Dipper is sprawled across the horizon and at its edge a dull, silver arc like a boat that has slipped its mooring, waiting to be pulled in, washed anew.

20 MPH

IT IS ANOTHER MINNESOTA morning warmed by Chinook winds, 7:40 a.m.: time to drop you at school. Just another day when the sky leaks daylight but the forecast says rain. I brace myself for the "not again" when I answer the phone. A DISH Network representative asks to renew your dead dad's subscription. *He's unable to come to the phone right now,* I say, my fingers spread out on his absence, a left-behind weight.

Eventually I get dressed, a ghost hiding between the folds. While driving, I go through a mental list of to-do items—change the AC and car filters, drop the pauses out of conversations, donate his clothes to the Salvation Army, change the pillowcase in your room because I hear you sob every night, when you're finding ways to fall asleep and there's no one to make chocolate milkshakes for you late at night, undo the dark or show you how to locate a thunderstorm on a radar map.

When the school signs come into view, I slow down to 20 mph, feel that quickening of pulse, wonder if I packed your lunch how your dad used to—two sandwiches, an eight-ounce chocolate milk carton, and a pack of banana chips from the bulk he ordered from Amazon. You are playing on your phone when I park next to the curb and look at you: overgrown hair covering the small of your neck, eyes looking beyond the windshield, and you make a fist that will guide you where they teach how to add or subtract your feelings, balance equations, and let your grammar sink and froth in its own errors. I say, *Have a good day*, but no sound comes out. You push your hands in your pocket, walk away, your face burning with questions.

I drive back, my feet a few centimeters away from the brake pedal as kids rush past, but more so because it's the way of our life—a yellow light inside always ready to go red, and all the distance I cover after returning home is going up and down the stairs while a part of me rattles, willing to break free from the muscles and gravity. When I cast slant glances upward at the same sky devoid of rain, finishing my tea, I realize that it is past July, and the cicadas haven't come this year. The silence drifts across the rooms, and through the bust of the screen door the patio is well lit with the bare neck of the sun. The bedsheets unlearn the language of your dad's body. I settle into my disquiet as an old man into his slippers. At lunch, I stare into the blue of the TV and, later, practice how I'll smile when I see you at 3 p.m., what I'll talk about: perhaps homework, the upcoming dentist's appointment, with slight concern in my voice.

And it's home again: another pizza takeout and three hours of TV while I fold the laundry, unclog the sink of tight-mouthed condescension, set the soil setting on the washer to heavy, start a fresh load that tosses and turns like we do every night. Then I think to write thank you notes to everyone who helped. Instead, I sit down with you and watch the movie you're watching because you want me to despite the dial of my mind pushed far left to empty, and a low beam is all we have between us that never gets me past the school driving limit even when the intersection is cleared, the forecast is right as rain, and no warning lights flash asking me to slow down.

STORM WARNINGS

I RETURN FROM WORK to find my teenage son sitting in the Jacuzzi tub in the master bathroom. "There was a tornado warning," he says, and shows the radar images on his phone: green and yellow waves, a cherry-red dot moving away from where we live, making me look harder after it swirls and disappears.

Upstairs, my mother calls my name, says she is hiding in her closet. The room is dark. I turn on the bedside lamp. "Come out, Ma, it's time for your medicine."

I hear the shuffle of her silk and chiffon saris, untouched for six months now. My mother feels comfortable in her kaftan—it's easier to sleep, use the bathroom, her bald head covered in a scarf. She opens the drawers in the dresser and her diamond earrings gleam in the dim light. My father's notebook of poems on the side. Feathers from old hats, a dead bug stuck between them.

"No toilet paper," my mother says.

I know there is, but I still check. She tells me someone steals it every day. I comfort her, it won't happen again. The hospice nurse has told me such hallucinations are common.

•

My husband calls from nine hundred miles away. "Are you okay?" he asks.

"The tornado touched down fifty miles from here." Pause. I hear the chattering behind him. "Are you there?"

He says he's waiting in line at a restaurant to get seated. Pause. "Anything else?"

"What's the appropriate age to stop kissing your son on the cheek?" I ask.

•

My son has put up a new poster, an active volcano in Sicily. He likes the smell and gloss of fresh paper until it gathers dust and is retired to the basement. Sometimes I go down and arrange his posters in a corner. The edges of mountains, oceans, plains rolled up against each other. The walls seem whiter, closer. Poster after poster, until I lose count.

When I come up, he is going back to his room, a grape soda in his hand. I ask him about his day at school. He closes his door.

•

Two days later, I bring a plant into my mother's bedroom, place it next to the windows. She smiles weakly, patches of balm on her lips.

Tofu curry and spinach for her. Keema aloo for my son. I roll out the bread thin and keep it soft so she can chew. My son takes dinner in his room; I can hear the keyboard clicks, the haste to reach the end point in a video game, the hurry to grow up. I feed my mother while she watches her favorite movie again. My mother is my child now.

•

One night, when I come in to turn off the lights in her room, my mother is wearing the diamond earrings, holding the book of poems. "The plant is a nice shade of green," she says. I kiss her goodnight.

The following afternoon, my son returns from school and says everyone in his class is white. He has just started eighth grade. We invite one of his friends and his parents for lunch, prepare spaghetti with meat sauce. "It's too spicy," they say, and leave a few minutes later, their forks still wrapped with curled food. My son is deflated, every chance of him being accepted as an American gone.

•

"Will you tell me a story?"

"Of course," I say, and snuggle with my mother, the lumpy stomach I always liked. Once again, she mentions I was born after almost ten months, longer than any baby she'd known. Her frail hands sit in between my hair. I tell her about when she met my father for the first time and immediately didn't like him; how I was conceived on a monsoon evening. It makes her giggle even though it's something I made up.

I press my palm against her cheek. She points to the wall next to the window, where I traced my father's silhouette one evening when he visited us—his head drawn longer than the rest of his body, his nose and forehead distinct as his voice.

"Do you remember when I caught you masturbating in the living room of our old home?" She imitates my jerky movements and starts laughing so hard her words disappear.

"Yes, and all I said in my defense was that it felt good." I join her laughter, our throaty sounds hitting the walls, bouncing back, stinging our eyes.

When we quiet down, she says she hasn't been the best mother. There were a couple rough years. I look at the ceiling and realize the fan is gray in color. "Who has a gray ceiling fan?" I blurt. My mother starts crying.

"I slept with another man while your father was alive," she sobs in between her words. I look at her face and place my hands over her shoulders. She wipes her tears with the sleeve of her kaftan. "You think it's easy doing the right thing?"

•

Last night's storm is over; a peach sky. I leave early for work so I don't run into women in their yoga pants, sucking their stomachs in, their fluorescent-colored sports bras rubbing the air around me. On one side of the bridge, a murky trickle consummates with a lake; on the other, white fences, ranch-style houses like a string of Polaroids on a clothesline. When I drive back home, the long-bellied clouds veil the sun.

Nighttime, I hover weightless in my dreams—nothing is expected of me anymore, I am as attractive as I can be. It's unlike a nightmare but close in the sensations of one. In front of the mirror, my slim torso bends forward to kiss my reflection.

•

A few weeks later, my son claims he has made a friend; he's learning a new language.

"What is it? Spanish, French? Hindi?" I grow hopeful toward the end of the multiple choices.

He laughs. "It's just a great place to hide words you don't approve of."

•

Indian Chinese takeout tonight. Bright red Manchurian masala, fried rice, Hakka noodles. My mother tastes a bit of everything, her tongue streaked orange and yellow, her eyes misted because of the spice. She looks like an Indian goddess. I fail with the chopsticks again.

•

Fortune cookies on our laps. Mine says: *Look for an opening.*

•

My husband walks around aimlessly in our home, rubbing his eyes. I notice how hairy his legs are. He's always looking over his shoulder as if he's afraid to miss something. His cell vibrates in his pocket. He moves away from me to his home office, closing the door behind him. I am tempted to listen in. Is he having an affair?

"Why are you outside Dad's office?" My son comes up behind me.

"It's nothing," I say gently, even though I am spooked. "I'm waiting to tell him something."

My son looks at me expectantly. "What is it?"

"It's about this coworker."

"Oh," he says, shrugs and walks away.

•

It's a long week at the hospital. My mother's body shrinking. Her cancer fuzzy and cloudy on her scans. I stay with her, stretched out on a chair by her bedside or on the bench against the window. She gives me her ring.

"Not now," I whisper and hand it back to her. She forces a smile and places it on my palm. I feel the weight of an *after* that will arrive when she's gone. I hug her for a long time, but it doesn't feel enough.

My mother passes away the following weekend. It's late autumn, the shadows at drowsy angles. I catch her face in a curious light before she's cremated. I wish to know her all over again, bashful, grinning.

I go into her room to give away her things. The drawers open like hours. The lull of the table lamp. I close my eyes and see her silhouette at the window watching a wing-heavy sparrow on the branch of a twisted cypress. Then she streams into the gaps between the heater vents and disappears. In my bedroom, I hang a framed picture of her. Colors in her eyes, behind her. She has been gone for a week.

Urn of her ash in my closet. Everything reduced to brown or black. Where does all the blood go?

•

The door to my son's room is open. He is playing an online game when I softly knock. He signals me to come in if I don't say a word. I sit on his bed and watch the jumping and crashing kids, the mine-fields, the sudden explosions, the fires and lightning on his screen, a storm of chaos and violence.

•

On a long car trip, I'm in the back, eating peanuts, crunching silence. The back of my husband's head a black blot in front of my eyes. "I am tired," he says. "I am exhausted," he repeats. When we stop at a gas station, he stands up like an old piece of machinery reluctant to start. Ahead of us, a lone cloud gauzing the sunset. The land around us pushed into the ground, barren. I watch my son walk with my husband.

On our way back, a gust slides across the roof and windows of our car, pushing past the trees on the roadside. I feel a tug, wanting to be swept away.

•

My husband buys Swarovski earrings on his next business trip. Trans-parent crystals, a rainbow inside each of them. He touches my fin-gertips with his as he places them in the palm of my right hand. Soft. Reassuring. "Duty free," he says, and smiles.

"Beautiful," I say and put them on. Little pieces of sky dangling from my ears.

He hums in his office. My son is in his room. My mother gone for months. The tick tock of the living room clock. I sit on the top of the stairs, the hardwood shifts, adjusts. Glancing at the picture frames along the slope of the white trim feels like looking at your life from a distance—lost radiance, chubbiness. I go into my mother's bedroom, curl up next to the hot vent.

•

Storm warnings again. I'm sitting in my tub, bubbles and bath bombs. A taste of salt on my tongue, yesterday's deodorant in my armpits. I rub my heel on the tub floor, call it home. Outside, the sky thunders. The rain taps on the roof, harder each subsequent time. The water makes a *glub glub* sound around the drain, the way it moves, each time a new eddy, an animal set loose from a cage. I watch it intently and forget what it means to share yourself with another.

SWALLOW

THE FIRST TIME I swallow a human face, the nose scratches my throat. I cough and gulp water.

"It takes practice," my senior coworker Nusrat says as she licks a face left behind by a teenage girl and removes a bill of one hundred dollars taped to it. Turquoise shadow on the half-opened lids, the thin forehead creases, the little circles of black under the lifeless eyes. Nusrat lets it slide, turning it around like a baby through the birth canal.

Nusrat has a large mouth, her lips open wide, wider than anyone I have seen. She loves faces of young men and women, except mustaches and beards. The hair gets tangled in her system and makes her gag and finally puke. The best part about swallowing a face is the words that linger at the edge of the lips or inside the cheek, they make a sound before they hiss and drown. The accent that stays on for days. Sometimes a foreign language.

"Mm," Nusrat says. "Cherries, this girl had cherries."

The faces I have been practicing on are of dolls, rubbery. They twist and turn, get pressed without much effort and pass out of my system with the right laxatives. Some faces are inedible, they have too much violence in their skin. It's best to bury those. Face-swallowing is a new eco-friendly way to support the evolving cosmetic industry, to avoid flooding the earth with bio waste. The money is decent given the risk. There is time off every few weeks to give our systems some rest.

"No one likes what they are born with," Nusrat says with a somber expression, her teeth flesh-stained, her lips cracked, fissured, wet. Radio comes on. Nusrat likes to hear music while we work. She pushes another face in her mouth. Her teeth swiftly get out of the way, her throat a gleaming hot-pink hole with white patches on her hard palate. I hear a light thud followed by a hiss, as if the face settled in her gut, released its memories of frowns and laughter, of shame and joy, the food it devoured, the taste it endured.

Nusrat confides she's been in love with a face, a face of a young woman. "I wish you could see the radium glow in her eyes, the sharp knife of her jawline. She must have been a model. My mind imagined her mouth on my nine openings, her pointed nose cartographed a new map on my body." Her voice cracks and deepens. "I kept her face on my bedroom windowsill for days. When it started rotting, I buried it in a flowerpot."

I turn my head, look at the slant of the evening light after the showers, the hill in the distance turning red like an exposed cheek in winter, above it a forehead of sky with faint creases of clouds.

"Everyone has a face—a mountain, a lake, a tree, a tiger, even the moon," Nusrat says. "To have a face is to want. To have a face is the beginning of a swallow by something bigger, uglier."

I ask her when she is going to retire. "Soon," she says. "The sores are getting worse," her face crimped with anxiety, at once impulsive and monstrous. "If anyone were to look down in my gut, it'd be a ghost tour, tiny pools of eyes and open lips, skin soft and thin like cheese, easy to spread."

I gulp a solution of laxatives and get ready for the next shift. The ground below my feet is wet, ready to mold. The air smells of tears, saliva, a sour breath. A few inches away, a bucket of water with baby waves. In the reflection, my face looks wrinkled, ancient, impossible to digest.

WHITE ASH

My wife, Ritu, a receptionist at a motel, works four nights a week. In the morning, I pick her up in our used Honda and drive her home. After she showers, I bring her a cup of fresh ginger and cardamom tea. She smells of lavender, her hair glowing with water beads, her eyelashes stuck together. In bed, she sips the tea without speaking, and I have the urge to ask how she is. I place my hand on her knee. She doesn't push my hand away like she used to, but I know she isn't fine. I am not fine. The silence between us is intolerable.

•

Six months ago, our four-year-old daughter went missing from her pre-K school playground. According to her teacher, she was playing with a doll behind the slide. When the kids lined up to go back to the lunchroom, the teacher realized our daughter wasn't on the playground. The doll was on the ground, face down in the wood chips. Since that day, each dawn cried her name on local TV and radio, posters on the walls, trees, and poles. *MISSING* printed on our foreheads, on our tongues, on our outstretched arms and running legs. We rushed into every shadow that approximated her size, drove around the city several times a day, very fast, and then slammed the brakes until we were out of breath.

"Did you find a new place for our posters?" Ritu asks, lying in bed, her eyes closed, trying to sleep.

"Yeah," I say, though I don't know of any.

"We need to keep trying."

"Do you want me to heat the rotis and cauliflower sabzi?" I ask, remembering she must be starving.

"I'm not hungry," she answers and brings the blanket up to her chin.

A few weeks back, I watched a program on the Discovery Channel about how long camels can go without food or water while roaming in the desert. Forty days. After our daughter was gone, we could go for only two and a half days without meals. A few weeks later, sleep returned with bursts of nightmares. Screaming in attics, basements, abandoned warehouses, woods, dirt under my nails digging up graves, finding a pair of old socks, a broken shoe, a torn piece of cloth from her dress. The doll lying face down in dirt, sometimes with our daughter's head.

I watch the slow rhythm of Ritu's body sinking into sleep, the vent above my head blowing hot, dry air. Everything is so quiet, it feels like an avalanche came over and buried us under it.

In the living room, I settle in my brown recliner and start the TV, keep it on mute. A feature on Chile's Miner Miracle. *68 days trapped half a mile underground*, the news ticker says. On the screen, reporters speak intensely, some people sob. My eyes mist and the images blur. I get up for a tissue. When my phone rings, I realize I am standing in the kitchen, staring at the cabinets, holes where the handles used to be. I don't remember opening them for a while now. They have rows of plastic bottles with red pepper flakes, cumin, ajwain, fennel, and mustard seeds. Turmeric and garam masala. Whatever brings taste to our food as we remember it from our home in India. My phone rings again. In a video call, my mother is staring at me. I close the apartment door behind me. Outside, it's freezing, but I don't want to wake up Ritu.

"Hello," my mother says twice, her voice overlapping the sound of a Hindi film song from the TV behind her.

"Namaste, Ma," I say in the most distant voice possible, as if reminding her I am far away—past the oceans, the continents.

"What's wrong?" she asks, intently looking at me. Her eyes look darker than they are in the grainy video. "Did you hear anything from the police?"

"No."

"Where's Ritu?" she asks.

"Sleeping." A white puff of air releases. On the street, three elementary school kids are walking to the bus stop, their mittened hands holding onto the straps of their bright backpacks.

"It has been two years since you left for America, son. You should come back now."

"I cannot come back to India, not right now. I don't know why you keep saying that."

Something in my voice sparks panic in her eyes. She clears her throat.

"Today is Shivaratri." She pauses. "Are you planning to fast?"

"I don't feel like it," I say, my finger hovering over the oval red *END* at the corner of my phone screen.

"Last year, Ritu made all the preparations for the fast, sabudana cutlets, potatoes in a curry of coriander and cumin. She sent pictures of the decorated temple in your home. And now I don't even see her," she complains.

"Ma, I have to go."

"It's because of this non-religious attitude you have so much suf-feri—"

I disconnect the call. My eyes stray upward to a rectangle of sky visible from where I stand, hoping to catch some colors of the morning. Instead, there is a thick ceiling of gray.

•

In the office, I pull out my laptop and power it on. Fifty unread emails. Mostly for the servers that went down last evening for maintenance. I start the diagnostic tests that should have been run yesterday. When I open my drawer for my notebook, I see a stack of posters of my daughter—her grainy black and white face, her dress with a bow from Macy's, a missing lower tooth. I cover them with other papers. One of my colleagues hollers my name from the corridor. A snoozed reminder on my computer goes off. These days, I am late for everything. Late coming into work, late to meetings, deadlines, late leaving from work, late to sleep. In the conference room, while everyone is discussing the status of the shutdown last night, I am looking at the tall windows. The snowfall has begun. Arcs of wind and flakes. Another day of reduced visibility, slow driving, tire marks stacked on the roads, some cars pushed to the side of the Schuylkill Expressway at odd angles. The world looks huge, infinite. *I am never going to find my daughter.* The same thought, every hour, minute, moment. Unrelenting. Her face hangs at the center of everything I see. Even after I close my eyes. It covers every pixel my mind touches. I wonder if I will ever see things as they are.

Someone says my name and I return to myself, spooked.

•

My friend Salil, who lives in a neighboring town, calls me on my lunch break. "We have satsang tonight. The priest from the Krishna temple in downtown Philly will be giving sermon. Why don't you and Ritu join us?"

"Ritu has a shift, I can't," I lie, knowing Ritu is off from work tonight.

"Ah, then you can come, na, after dropping her?"

"This weather is not great for driving, and you know I still get confused at night with exits."

"Hmm." He pauses. "I thought it might be good since you are… you know what I mean, right?"

"Sorry, Salil, maybe next time."

"Sure, sure. I have sent you an email, in case you change your mind. You should google this priest, he is a renowned man, great knowledge of scriptures. He also has a YouTube channel. Preeti and I listen to him every day."

"How is Preeti?"

"Recovering. You know how these things are. Sometimes I think we're in the same boat," he says.

"How so?"

"I mean, you lost your child, we keep going through these miscarriages."

"It's not the same." The words fall out of my mouth like loose coins. In that moment, I imagine Salil's soft, cheerful face, a head full of hair, and a tendency to argue, and my urge to prove to him that my grief is deeper, is stronger, because it's simply mine.

"I understand, but sadness is sadness, you know what I mean?" Salil wants to continue talking.

"Hey, I've got to go, am late for a meeting."

I stare at the blank screen of my phone for a few minutes. Even though I have been sitting on this chair for the past hour, I feel suddenly displaced.

•

When I reach home at 6 p.m., Ritu walks out of the bedroom like a ghost, her hair tangled, her eyes red. I drop a sheaf of mail on the kitchen counter without a glance.

"Why aren't you distributing her pictures somewhere?" Her voice is sharp with anger, since she knows my office day usually ends at five thirty and I must have driven straight home, given the inclement weather and the traffic at this time on US 30.

"There's nowhere else." I try to stay calm. I let the strap of my laptop bag slide from my shoulders and leave it on the dining room chair.

I walk over to her and take her in my arms. She pushes me and walks away.

My phone chimes. It's a WhatsApp message from Salil: *Here is the discourse for tonight's satsang*, it says. I scroll to the bottom of the long message to thank him and pause at the last line.

In the end, somehow, you get through everything. Anything.

•

At night, Ritu is dressed in a two-sizes-too-large sweater with skinny jeans and snow boots, her powder-blue purse hung on her shoulder, ready for her shift. Her hair is up in a bun, uneven gloss on her lips. Standing next to the kitchen wall, she looks like a house fixture, an absence.

"Did you know today's Shivaratri?" Her tone sharp, accusing. "We should have prayed, we should have made offerings, we should have—"

"I thought you are off from work today." I cut her off, unintentionally.

For a moment, Ritu looks around as if trying to find a place to bury her forgetfulness and anger. Then she goes back to the bedroom and locks it from inside.

In the kitchen, I heat up naan. The butter melts quickly on the naan's uneven surface and collects in the ridges on the bread. Cauliflower tastes undercooked, so I slice a leftover peeled onion, mince two cloves of garlic, and add some oil in a pan. As the cumin seeds scatter and fry in the hot oil, I add onion slices and garlic, toss the florets in it. Through the kitchen window, the sky looks like a mushy pillow. From the corner of my eye, I catch a little wooden pony moving due to heat blowing from a nearby vent, at the edge of the dining room wall. The toy wasn't there in the morning when I left. Maybe Ritu took it out from the toy chest where I kept all the toys away from our eyes. I watch the pony move back and forth, and my appetite fades like its slowing movements. I pick it up and shove it at the bottom of the trash can and stare at the garbage—stale onion peels, used paper napkins. Five minutes later, I take the pony out and wash it. Wipe it and put it back where I found it. By the time I return to the cauliflower sabzi, it has burnt dark, a waft of smoke rising from the pan.

•

It's past eleven when Detective Roberts calls. "We want you to come down to the station and look at something."

"Yes, of course," I say, instead of asking him, *Did you find her? A part of her? Anything?* I sit at the edge of my bed, my blanket lumped in my lap.

"Who was that?" Ritu asks, her eyes struck with ache and sleep.

"We need to go to the station."

On our way, the snow has turned thick, white ash from the sky. Large flakes stick to the windshield and slip with nothing to hold onto. Mounds of snow on the sidewalk.

When we reach the parking lot, Ritu says, "I want to stay here for a few minutes."

I put the car in park, engine running. A part of me wants to rush inside, a part of me never wants to go in. She takes my hand and presses it.

"I never saw a snowfall before I came to the US," she says.

"Me neither," I say gently.

"It's like flowers falling from the sky until they hit the ground and become dirt. Some slow, some too fast. That's the journey, isn't it? From above to down here."

I watch her face. It looks round but not so full anymore, the mole on her upper lip prominent under the fluorescent streetlight, her eyes narrowing at the dark extending past the windshield of our car. I'm ready to step out when she places her hand over mine, a soft sound slicing the snow-lit silence. We are looking at the night's eye and it's not gone but less likely to swallow us whole.

Face down, the sky continues to shred as if it understands the grief and rage of losing. Of living.

POTHOLES IN THE SKY

MY FATHER CLEANED THE Mumbai city gutters during the day and dug our backyard at night. He said he was looking for a treasure that my grandfather buried before he died. On his breaks, my father sat under the banyan wiping his sweat with the edge of his undershirt, worms curled around his wrists, mud stuck to his fingers. I brought him snacks and water from the house. When he got up, he pinched my ninth-grade, calcium-deficient cheeks and went back to digging with the confidence of someone not risking anything, not even his sleep.

"After you dig out something, you cleanse it of its previous life. Those are the rules of excavating," my father said. He pulled a doll, naked, a magenta pout, her hair golden or what was left of it. Her eyes staring as if widened by the thin tint of the night. After washing the doll from a garden hose, I draped her in an old kitchen rag and named her Janaki—she birthed from the earth like Sita, wife of Lord Rama.

Inside our home, my mother binge-watched an old soap on the TV. In between, she pulled the curtain to check on my father and frowned that he didn't look at her. The idea of digging appealed to her because everything existed in duality—wealth and misfortune, life and death. Often, she ran her fingers over the white, untanned bands on her left arm from her gold bangles, the ones she sold at a pawn shop to buy one month's rations when Father was laid off from his job at the municipality.

During his breaks, my father talked about the shit he cleaned during the day—the underbelly of a metropolis lined with rats, cockroaches. How he saw specks of gold amidst the dust and grime of Zaveri Bazaar. How he was a part of a rescue operation when a two-year-old fell in one of the open potholes in Dadar, a suburb.

"To dig is to locate a past," he said. "To dig is to connect with its suffering."

"Did the kid survive?" I asked.

He got up as if startled by the hanging roots of the banyan, swaying like ghosts in a pre-monsoon breeze. "If someone dug the sky, moons, galaxies, suns would fall out," he said, pointing at the smog-thickened ceiling. "Those glorified things up there," my father paused for a moment, "are the potholes of the sky."

I bit on the hard candy I'd carried in my pocket for weeks, the citrus sugar coating my tongue before falling into the pit of my gut, and wondered what passed down from my father to me. His hands, his urge to dig, and how he fit into this ping-pong of life and death. We were all in a hole of night, trying to come out clean from our past lives, our history dense around us like mud. Whirls of humid air climbed like a ladder. Something in the banyan moved, possibly a bird.

On Diwali night, my father took a break from digging. He washed the copper idols of Laxmi and Ganesh, lit two ghee lamps. My father wore a white, starched kurta pajama, a red shawl on his left shoulder. My mother smelled of kerosene and spices, frying puris and fluffing the boiled rice with her long hair pinned, the pallu of her red gota sari wrapped around her back and stuffed into her waist. The front door was kept open to welcome Laxmi. We took turns watching the door, the chilled breeze waking me when I dozed off. The lamps burned to the last drop of ghee, illuminating our hopes, and finally dying out, wicks charred like the new moon night.

The more my father dug, the deeper he wanted to be, as if he was like a man who just broke a lifelong fast and didn't know when to stop eating. He stopped going to work and started on a different patch, his bare feet pressing on the loose soil, pushing him in. He rarely came inside the house, the night hollow around him. He said he could put his ear to the ground and hear voices whispering, guiding him. He was certain there was a treasure waiting for him, like a secret to be unearthed, acknowledged, and admitted. The mounds rose—hills decorated with splayed weeds and exposed earthworms, little flags on the dirt, wrinkled and soft as a newborn's skin. I kept Janaki on the side of the fence watching him.

There were notices from his offices, unpaid bills piling on the kitchen table. My mother warmed up food for him and it went cold. She warmed it up again, adding water to the curries, until she threw them away.

"Your father looks like a demon," she said, as I sat down to eat with her.

"How long until you stop?" she yelled through the kitchen window, drawing the curtain that had become a partition between them in the hope that if she didn't see him, she would cease to believe he existed.

"Until the earth has returned everything it took from me." He laughed. Foam fell from his mouth. His yellow-stained teeth shone like gold from the darkness they were rooted in.

BARELY FORMED

In the bathroom mirror that night, the man looked through his eyes into his forehead for a long time. He was a forty-year-old car salesman in a small town and had managed to be the employee of the month twice in a row ten years ago. His biggest accomplishment was that he owned a Chevy truck and a navy suit.

Lying next to his wife, the man tried to sleep. From the window, the night gaped, absent of the moon, a pure darkness leeching from outside. His hands brushed her belly, his fingers on her exposed stomach, the slight depression near her navel moving with her breath. He felt he saw inside the dark of her body: a myriad of capillaries, bones threaded with empty sacs, a half-animal and half-human creature in her womb. The baby with its barely formed eyes looked at him and smiled.

How did this happen? They never planned on having a baby. He looked into the dark again, tried to make his mind blank. He had no business being a father. What if he attached his thoughts to the fetus and it stopped growing? The umbilical was twisting and untwisting around the baby's body. Both the cord and the baby were moving slowly, as if swimming in a gentle sea, lapped in waves. He felt ashamed of what he did and closed his eyes. He could hear a chord strumming, a faint voice singing. It felt as if he was in outer space, and the baby, nothing but a big head and a mound of flesh and limbs attached to it, was holding onto him. They were a part of an endless song.

The man imagined renovating the second bedroom, making a crib. Soft murmurs on a baby monitor. Murals on the bare, pastel walls. The toys and the bedtime stories. The bliss and the heartache that'd grow side by side while raising a child. The feats of strength he and his wife would be expected to perform. Eventually, the baby would grow up, tall with broad shoulders and large wrist bones, unlike him, and restore their house, take care of them, fall in love, father a bunch of cheerful kids. And now older, the man would become less and less likeable to his son, especially after losing his wife to an illness he cannot name right now. They'd argue and the man would say, "You don't understand." His son would say the same until, one day, he would place the man's frail, dead body in an oak-lined coffin. And speak at his funeral with a genuine politeness despite their differences. In times when his son would be alone, he would cry knowing that he was growing unlikeable to his own children.

The man was still drifting in the dark, listening to the singing, when he felt a pressure in his chest like he was going to burst. He realized a thought had escaped, something had made it real. He could feel himself reforming, empty and light. The darkness in his head receded like a fading pain. When he opened his eyes, his fingers were still closed around his wife's navel as if gathering all the hope, holding a soul. Moths tapped against the glass windows. The night had fallen and scattered as dew. Glancing at her glittering skin, the man wondered if the pattern inside the baby's head matched the one inside his, if the baby would do things the man wanted to do. If in the distant future, this baby, then a man lying next to his sleeping wife, would decide that they'd have the baby, of course they wanted the baby, the baby is exactly what they need.

SING ME A HAPPY SONG

THE SKINNY BOY MEETS the Devil in the elevator, on his way down. Woolen jacket and corporate smile, a warm halo around the black disk of his head, his unrepentant eyes glowing green. He asks the skinny boy about his day. The skinny boy clears his throat, says he's been running errands for his boss. When they step out, the day is cold like truth.

Back in his studio next to the train station, the Devil's voice sings in the skinny boy's head. It tugs at a part of him: the desire, the adventure. "Pay attention to your food," his mother says as she serves him dinner, her face ashen as ever since his dad left her. She collects her tears and prayers in a tall jar.

Manhattan is a showgirl at this hour. In the Devil's apartment, the skinny boy opens the Devil's closet, runs his fingers on the black and gray suits, sees his face on the surface of the shoes. The Devil is on the phone, his eyes on the boy, his voice low, firm. That night, the skinny boy feels the thrust of a grown man. A burning takes root, but he likes the torture. In the middle of the night, he sees the Devil standing next to the window, his back scaled like a reptile. A pair of wings below his blades. As the Devil flies out of the window, the skinny boy closes his eyes, shivering, scared. He imagines what his mother might say. "Sing me a happy song."

The Devil keeps a lock of the boy's hair in his pocket. The boy leaves his low-level job, watches the Devil interacting with his Wall Street clients, closing deals, offering them women and booze. Exotic animals. The moans and the music. How the Devil looks into their eyes, fills their voids and claims their light. They mistake it for living well, they were so unhappy before.

The boy is no longer skinny. His teeth feel sharper than before. The Devil swaddles him in a suit, buys AirPods. The boy visits his mother rarely. When he does, he tells her that her food tastes like shit. "I pray for you," she says and gives him a stuffed toy from his childhood.

The boy feels different every time he visits the Devil. The Devil speaks in poetry, teaches the boy to stay awake for days. "No one will ever love you enough except the night," he says. From the high-rise, the boy glances at the rush-hour traffic, the pillars of the overpass glowing red in the sunset, holding the weight of the ungrateful world as it spins faster and faster. He feels the vibrations in the walls and the floor. His animal-hungry eyes can see for miles, the wind hissing in and out of his lungs, his steps sensing the dead, their skulls crushed and mixed with dirt and concrete.

The boy visits his mother one night. She doesn't offer him food because she says he's a picky eater now. When he's about to leave, she warns him of the dangers ahead, her wrinkled walnut face twisted with discomfort. A train goes by, throwing the jar of tears on the floor. Prayers bubble out.

"Do you still love me?" the boy wants to ask, but his words loiter at the back of his throat, their tiny, sweaty feet fumbling. "I forgive you," she says, and asks him to leave.

The Devil is waiting in the lobby when the boy arrives. The boy has always loved the Devil's aftershave smell. They sit on the warm floor of the Devil's bedroom. He places his lips on the boy's mouth,

feeds him his tongue, sucks out the remaining faith. He gets a blind-
fold, a scarf and handcuffs, whispers the safe word in the boy's ears.
The sharp angles of the metal push against the boy's wrists. The pain
feels genuine and swift, carries him through the small hours of the
night. The shove of violence.

When the boy wakes, the window is open like a cracked egg,
and the Devil is gone, the apartment empty of furniture and belongings. It's quiet like death. From the corner of the room, the stuffed
toy stares at him, mouths grief. The boy sees his rippling shadow,
his back stiff, blazing, the feathers sprouting and catching wind, the
scales stretched like skin.

EARTH'S TEARS

SITTING ON MY PATIO sofa, a bright flash on a new moon night, cotton furry clouds stuck to her long, shimmery dress, my girlfriend from Venus threatens to disappear if I take her name.

"The world does not need another name," she writes a note, passes it to me. A smiley face at the end.

My girlfriend's hair is golden, her eyes are the greenest thing. She's thin as a summer rain. Sometimes her breath fogs up the air around her.

We trade our jeans, shop online. I eat my kale salad; she drinks her protein. Her ears twitch sensing my chewing, my gulping. Her sharp jawline cuts the evening in half. Afterward, she grabs the keys to my truck. Like a bug, I follow her.

In the parking lot she makes out with me, her perfume a shot of intergalactic scents I can breathe in all night. We drive around in the dark, playing her favorite music. My truck with all the glitter looks like a traveling hip-hop band. We watch the moon waxing, waning, as there isn't one orbiting Venus.

"Conversation is for people who do not understand each other," she wrote down in our first meeting. Over time, we've gotten the hang of it, though I wonder if we'll break up because of being bored of not saying something that might hurt one another.

At home, she plants a few seeds, watches them grow. She sleeps with her hands stretched out, as if the universe is taking a dip in her dreams. She picks up rocks from my backyard, puts them in a Ziploc bag, labels them "Earth's Tears."

I hide one pair of her glasses, a pair of panties, a hair clip. She doesn't look for them, like she planned to leave them behind. I rub her shoulders, braid her hair. We swim, we jump into new silences punctuated by blowing bubbles or sniffles.

In my kitchen, there is a poster of Venus. With a red Sharpie, she marks all the places she has been. They look like footprints. Before she leaves, we sit down in meditation. I guess it's supposed to make our separation bearable. There are tears deep in my gut when I imagine breathing in her scent, breathing in her dreams, breathing in the imagined sound of her voice, breathing in and out, then just out, out.

When she's gone, it takes a few days for the sound of my voice to come back. I unearth the nouns, the verbs, water her plants. "Please, please," I say in front of the mirror, "don't go," her name buried down my throat, her strange spectacles on the bridge of my nose showing a stretched, elongated version of me. My hands are callused adjusting the telescope, my eyes twitch visualizing her gazing at the space, holding the Earth's Tears in her palms, but all I see is a dry surface with rolling planes covered with old lava flows, mountains, and volcanoes. At nights, sometimes I drive out to a nearby beach, my feet submerged in water touching and receding, leaving salt, smaller rocks. The waves are noisy. Venus is bright white in the shining dark sky, as big as a doll head, and I walk toward it, raise my finger to touch it. And somewhere in that endless waiting and uncountable space between us, she sends a heart emoji with an echo effect. It floods the dark screen of my device with a luxuriant red, momentarily beats through the speakers.

GROUND ZERO

THE DAY BABRI MASJID in North Central India is demolished, I realize I'm pregnant. The television in my dorm community hall is a blaring horn of Hindu activists at the demolition site in Ayodhya, about nine hundred kilometers from the university town. Slogans on raised saffron flags, bandanas with *OM* written on them. They are shouting, *Ram, Ram,* and it does not sound holy, but like a warning sign that anything can happen. Back in my room, I make a mental note of my last menstrual cycle—two weeks late. I press my stomach; it bounces back with a light flab and roundness to it. Or maybe I am looking too hard at it. When I step into the corridor, a girl rushes past announcing that the city is under curfew until dawn. Our zip code has a mix of Hindu and Muslim families, and there's a possibility of a riot breakout.

My eyes cast out of the window, my mind elsewhere. The streets are deserted except a body of winter fog under the streetlights, until a series of vehicles with police sirens fill the air with dust and commotion. There's an announcement in the hallways to assemble in the community hall.

"No one is allowed to go outside," our hostel warden says, "until the situation is in control."

"When will that be?" someone asks.

"I don't know at this point," the warden answers and hurries away. Some girls climb the stairs to the fourth-floor terrace to get an overview of the neighborhoods. Now on mute, the TV displays hundreds of Hindu fundamentalists standing next to the debris that was a place for prayer in another century, an artifact of history. I glance at the bright red Hindu thread on my wrist, something my mother tied before I left home for college. My tummy rumbles. My palm is glazed with sweat.

Staring at the calendar, I try to remember when Manu, my classmate, and I last fucked. Was it in that unfinished, abandoned building behind our favorite restaurant? My back scratched against the exposed brick wall while his feet slid on the sand, trying to stay in position. Our whispers and moans boomeranged off the roof and rose as dust. Was it the cheap motel with a shitty bed, next to the bus depot far away from our university? Was it because I inhaled all his lust, sitting twenty feet away from him in a robotics class?

During the day, the city opens for several hours, so I request the gatekeeper to send a message to Manu, who lives in a boys' hostel half a kilometer from where I am. In the next hour, Manu and I are outside a clinic. Before the gynecologist, we pretend to be married, and because of being full-time students, and having no financial independence, convey our unwillingness to have a baby.

"Whatever happened to guarded intercourse?" The doctor asks something to that effect while performing an internal exam. *It's not the same.* I want to repeat Manu's words, but I stay quiet while she scolds me like my mother. I should have resented her, but hundreds of miles away from my parents, it feels right and satisfying. "If you are not pregnant," she says, "your period will arrive after finishing this course," and hands me a prescription. I stare at it hard, memorizing the spelling of the medicine. In my head, there is a misunderstanding in my body, a wrong calculation in my bio cycle.

At the pharmacy, a live reporter on TV is canvassing the scene after a riot. Corpses of over one thousand Hindus and Muslims killed so far. The images of dust-ridden bodies, half-opened eyes, their empty palms facing the sky. They look the same—forlorn, frightened, the creases deep on their foreheads, pathways of beliefs that divided them. The ground makes no distinction based on their religious beliefs. Walking back, Manu tries to hold my hand and I push it away. Part of me resents him, and part of me knows we are both to blame. He kicks an empty can on the unpaved road, but it doesn't go far. The grass on the playground is yellow and dry. So much is slaughtered around us, but I'm building a life. Maybe. Maybe not.

The sunlight comes smashing into my room without any regard for the dead or the alive. I feel a slight wetness between my legs and let out a sigh of relief. Perhaps my body needed a pill to kick it back into its natural rhythm. Perhaps everything will be fine. Perhaps the riots will stop today. I walk slowly to the bathroom as if I don't want the wetness to be sucked back in, as if I need to see it before it flushes in the toilet, as if a part of me needs proof that something is, indeed, not growing in me amidst all that un-want, un-desire, unlove I feel. Inside the bathroom, I find it's a transparent discharge. A cry escapes my lips and I fist-bomb my abdomen. *Leave me,* I whisper so the girl in the next stall doesn't hear me, my angst morphing into the clattering of my teeth and the shaking of my body, my sour morning breath filling the space around me. In the minutes, hours, and days to come, I anxiously wait for a stain, but there's still no riot between my legs. Instead, blood is spilled on the streets, the lockdown longer. In the dining hall, a national newspaper shows a picture of a kar sevak proudly holding a broken brick from the fallen structure, his arms covered in dust and ash, his saffron bandana muted like a sun about to die.

Given the constraints of the curfew, it takes a few days to schedule the procedure. In the clinic, while I am prepared, I hear the doctor talking to Manu in another room—instructing him where to put his initials, his full name and contact address. Father of my child, my husband, my caretaker. I think it's strange asking him to give consent on my behalf when I am awake and listening. But I know he is doing as told. He is as scared and confused as I am. A nurse shaves my pubic hair, and I feel like ground zero, razed, a small black heap on the ground like dead ants that once crawled on my skin, filled me with muddy desire. Later, far away from the pile of Babri mud and chalk, I go in and out of consciousness, I hear a suction—a soul pulled away.

On our way back to my hostel, despite the cold, I'm sweating as if I have escaped narrowly from a crime scene. When I stare at Manu's face, he looks away, avoiding my gaze. Perhaps he's crying. Perhaps he's looking for a spot to bury his wordlessness. He is twenty, I am nineteen, and now we have something unspeakable between us. For the next few days, we don't meet, we don't pass messages to each other, we halt being us. When we come face to face in a grocery store on campus, he forces a smile and raises his hand to say hello, but my legs feel too weak to rush into his silhouette, my arms too scrawny to overcome the anxiety I feel. It seems like our days together have come to an end. I wake up late, I hardly eat. I watch the news, I look at the demolition site and think of my mopped womb. For hours I try to come up with the sound of loss. If it's the pounding of hammers and grappling hooks bringing down a sixteenth-century mosque. If it's the swipe of a blade against the throat of a child of a different faith, his shriek so distinct in the slogan-shouting mob. If it's the quiet hum of an operation theater or the clank of the instruments on the surgical tray, stained with a life that once was.

In the cold darkness of the nights, alone in my bed, the word abortion cuts my tongue in half. I try to keep Manu at the edge of my thoughts, not let him cut through the fence of my mind and penetrate my body. I try to sleep and dream of a clean place, a clean faith, a love unblemished by desire. Our bodies without the skin tainted of our memories. Do we ever cleanse? Does the dirt ever get tired of absorbing the mortar and the bricks, the bones and blood of the dead? Does it ever pause and wish for the healing to begin? No, the dirt goes on. And the sound of loss sinks deeper into the earth and echoes forever.

A cramp arises and I almost let out *Hey Ram*, a god I have known all my life but don't recognize anymore. The sound that once was of redemption is now buried under the rubble of the Babri. I pray it resurfaces while I toss and turn, my body rough on the sheets, resisting to let go what is left of Manu in me.

STRANGER AND THE GREEN GLOVES

ON A SUNDAY EVENING, when the early summer sky glittered like steel struck with light, a man came through their front gate and kissed the boy's mother. It was a few months after his father's death. She was on her knees working in the front yard, pulling weeds from the lawn. It was a hot day. Flies were persistent and buzzing. A clean rivulet of sweat ran down her neck. She had been quite oblivious and had not noticed her teenage son. He stood near the half-curtained window with his fingers laced together over his gray T-shirt, staring at the apostrophes of little black birds. And for the same reason as she felt the need to look at her shadow from time to time, she turned around and saw the man. She moved the damp hair away from her bronzed face and stood where she was. The man took her in his arms with a strange intimacy and kissed her pale lips, sliding her gloves to the side. They talked in a hushed tone. Then he left, leaving a slight tremor in the wind and a wet cloud in her eyes. The boy looked away as if it never happened.

In the days to come, she washed the gloves and kept them in a safe, cool corner. Her bare hands moved inside the mounds of dirt, synchronized to the pulse of earth as if something was sprouting within her. She worked all day and showered in the evening—her wet hair crimped in place with bobby pins and a small rose on the side. The flowers in her garden bloomed and collapsed as sacred verses in the lap of gravity; the streams of sun played Morse code in their kitchen, and as days turned into a haze, she lost track of time. The boy caught her sitting next to the washing machine long after the cycle had ended. Sometimes she stood next to the boiling milk until it stuck to the pan and turned brown. She kept the curtains drawn, the rosebush trimmed so she could oversee the entrance. Her ears picked up every sound—when a footstep hit the patio or when a spoon dropped or a bird took flight. She rarely slept, and when she did, she kept her knees close to her chest to get through the night.

The boy thought of saying something but never found the words beyond: "Mom, are you okay?"

"Yes, sweetie," she said. And he held her hand, his eyes reading her face, bare and concentrated.

After an uneventful summer and fall, the prismatic landscape changed to a banal gray. She spent more time by the fireplace, stuck on the same page of a romance novel, watching the snow cover her barren flowerbed, the gilded grass, and her hopes with an icy blanket.

When spring arrived, a heady smell of grass persisted for days. On the day exactly a year since the stranger had appeared, she sat amidst new bags of mulch and topsoil. Then, as if she recalled something, she recovered the green gloves from the corner and stuffed them in a half-filled trash bag. The boy, standing not too far away, snatched the shiny black bag and ran to the dumpster at the end of the street and emptied it over a heap of debris and circling flies. Then he climbed inside and mixed it until the gloves were out of sight. Knee-deep in filth, he looked at the sky. The sharp lines of light crisscrossed under the liquid blue canvas. Not a single cloud.

•

Holding one of the edges of the dumpster as though it were a close friend, he wept. His voice eventually faded until he could only hear its echo in his heart. When he arrived at home, he stood at the gate for a moment. His mom, with her back toward him, kneading the lumps of soil with her hands, sang lightly as if to a bird.

IT'S CRUCIAL WHERE YOU
HANG THAT MIRROR

ON THE BLUE-GREEN WALL that faces the backyard, catching the glimpse of red, yellow-streaked butterflies, moths, the scales of living and wild. Pink sky mauled by electricity, jet streams. In the afternoons, a dinosaur struggles to fit in your overgrown lawn, with gaps in its memory, centuries wide. Its blood has fertilized the earth, giving way to lush weeds, fragrant and hostile. Here and now, it has broken its own rule of existence. Despite its crisp reflection, you refuse to see it, just because it can't be, it can't be.

•

Next to the painting of produce above the pantry, where you have put the curtain on drugs, old recipes. A row of cookie jars, a loaf of bread, old pickles, making you hungry. A spider in the corner weaving, making up its mind. You gorge on a peanut butter sandwich; your hair looks wild. Dishes in the sink. The handprint of your son on the refrigerator door, amidst magnets in the shape of New Jersey, Oklahoma, California. Something snaps within you. The five-burner stove where you heat water, trying to remember the hard joy of doing something, anything, that utterly consumes you.

•

On the bare, mauve bedroom wall, grabbing the first light of the day, your lover's sweat-soaked head resting like a dark planet on your chest, her body a warm river where you drown, never coming up for love. Her darkened eyes, and how she laughs low in her throat and struts in heels before you fuck her with her clothes on. Your grip on her complete abandon of control, opposite to her rhythm, to cancel it out. A dust-ridden wedding picture on the nightstand, from where your dead wife watches your hair turning gray while she continues to look young and radiant.

•

In the corridor, the mirror flashes the wood panels of the front door, the treetops in your yard, a bird wrapping your house in a shrill sub-song, the nameless FedEx delivery guy. Glimpses of the wind chime shuddered by crosswind or the ghosts of your past slipping in. Their cold breath on your skin when you get up in the middle of the night, unable to sleep. Passing by the hole of light from the mirror, you walk slow, you wish you could hug your younger self and emerge as someone furiously new.

•

In the bathroom, where you land several times in a day, aroused or tired. Stepping out of a shower, or taking a call, sexting, a smug look that says no one can destroy you, work or personal, you have a status of doing things well. It's incredible, you say out loud and grin, as you trim your nails and shave. Until your eyes glint with sadness when you think of the dinosaur that refused to go extinct, and now, in a gilded frame, disintegrates in its own reflection.

MOTHER, LOST

THE TRAIN IS LOST. Halted in the middle of a grassland, it seems no one knows where we are. Ma says the clouds have shot the sun so it's hard to tell the time of day or the direction. I gaze at the string of rail-cars disappearing into the horizon as if searching for their beginning. Ma raises the glass window, coal and sand on the sill. Papa's standing outside on a grass patch next to our coach, the smoke from his cigarette blurring his face. Ma flings her hand through her long hair, knots it into a bun, raises a bottle of water to her mouth. I watch the water disappear in the tunnel of her neck, the fake pearl necklace (because we're traveling in a train) shifting on the edge of her collarbone.

We are traveling back from Ma's sister's wedding, where everyone dressed up and group-danced. Papa drank with the men and chewed on roasted cashews and fried fish. Someone spilled a drink on his suit, but he kept smiling and cleaned up with a wad of tissues, white bits stuck to his dark fabric like small wings. He shrugged a lot. Ma claimed he did it not to upset anyone by having an opinion, the cherry-colored henna on her palms and up to her elbows glittering just like the bride's. I was having my period, so I stayed with my grandmother, who rested on a diwan in a corner since her knees were recently replaced. Uncles and aunts who resembled Ma and who didn't stopped by to check on Grandma and pat my head, a few squeezed my cheeks—look how tall you are now, or we saw you when you were a baby, or what grade are you in, beta? And I leaked a little, felt a blot on the pad each time.

On the train floor, I see a butterfly, its upper wings ashen brown, bearing sickle moons of gold. The undersides flicker between green and bronze like Ma's earrings. I want to grow up beautiful and gloomy like Ma. Everyone pays attention to you when you are lost in your world. At home, Papa keeps following Ma, and she goes about her day like it's nothing.

A hawker comes by with packets of biscuits and cold drinks. Ma signals him to go away but he stays for a few seconds, a cola bottle condensing in the grip of his fingers. Ma shakes my shoulder, and I immediately regret staring at the cold drink. She has this way of looking at me that I feel I must apologize for wanting. In the distance, the clouds are shapeshifting. Switchblade light and sound explosions. A few seats away, a little girl keeps bubbling with her saliva.

Outside, the light dims quick like fast-forwarding a movie. Mostly I'm waiting for the train to move, the first push that will startle me, so my fear of being stuck here forever remains unspoken the way Ma doesn't talk about the names she picked for the baby who didn't live—he had a hole in his heart. Papa says at idle times like these we leaf through all our failures. I stare at his silhouette in the darkening day, trying to understand what it means. If he's thinking he should have married someone other than Ma. If he's forced to love me no matter how careless I am, like when I lost the LED from his circuit board or accidentally solved a quadratic equation on the margins of his research paper. Ma calls out to Papa to come inside, but he keeps pacing with the flashlight of his phone turned on, his face tinged blue. Everything looks thinner—the train, the buzzing green of the grass blades growing black as the night, Papa, as if pressed in the dark between the pages of a book. Ma peels an orange. Her fingers tug the white strands from the segments, dig the seeds out like a secret. She passes a slice. I suck on it and watch the curled rinds, the threads and a handful of white buds, broken, separate, something that was once snug and protected.

"Isn't it good?" Ma asks, her crimson lips stained with juice.

"Delicious," I say, and pick up another orange, rip it apart.

SOFT, HARMLESS MONSTERS

A FEW MONTHS AFTER my parents died, they appeared at my bedroom door, wobbling as if trying to stand on their broken frames. All I could see was half a face, a bulging eye, an open mouth like a wet hollow in a fig, parts of skull shining white when the air from my ceiling fan hit their loosely held bones, a smoke rising through their vertebrae. I was startled and happy to see them even though Ma had a smell like char, a faint trace of sweet talcum powder she used to apply after her bath, dried lacto calamine lotion settled in her fingernails. Papa smelled like dirt—damp and fermenting. Ma was wearing lipstick, just like the kind she had on when the accident happened. Papa's suit was torn in places, a bone sticking out of his elbow.

My fingernail grazed Ma's arm. The first touch was a jolt. The nail was rounded and trimmed, but Ma said it felt like a knife on her ruptured skin. After all these months of loneliness in the house, I didn't want to let go of the vertiginous tingling in my chest, but Ma pulled her hand back, shooing me away. "It's not safe for us, not yet," she said.

I stepped back and my parents moved around, limping. The edges of their skin, pale, thin, blending into the air.

"Guddi, I'd like some tea," Ma said.

I brought her hot water with an old, shriveled teabag crimped at the bottom of the cup.

"Never offer such a hot beverage to anyone," Ma said. "Might burn the lips." Papa laughed. A tooth hung at the corner of his mouth, a white speck in a dark abyss.

"We missed you, Guddi," Papa said.

"It took a while, but it's good to be back," Ma said and bared her front teeth, a stain of lipstick on one of them.

"Where have you been all this time?"

"We're still in-betweens because you haven't dispersed our ashes yet."

"Ma, I was supposed to go to Banaras with Viren uncle, but he backed out at the last minute. He said something about visiting the holy city later with his family, and I could join him then."

"We begged Viren not to go with you," Papa said, "so we could come back in some shape or form that you could recognize. Once the ashes are in the River Ganga, who knows where our limbs and heads will end up. They could be attached to different rocks, or in a fish's stomach."

"That's the intention, isn't it?" I said. "To start over?"

"Do you want us to leave you alone, Guddi?" Ma sneered, like I'd disappointed her again, not with poor grades or with the choice of boys I liked throughout high school, but with something more severe and unforgivable.

•

Weeks later, the monsoon rushed in after a long, dry summer, and the yard buzzed with rain, mosquitoes, and grumbling frogs. Ma, Papa, and I watched the lightning rip the sky—a bright, blinding buzz, the crack of thunder so loud it rattled the door and windows and the bones in my body. Ma and Papa rushed outside in the gray, jaundiced light, the wind slapping their silhouettes like prayer flags on a thin string. They screamed like excited kids.

"Come inside," I yelled, worried about their dangling frames in the whipping air.

Ma stormed indoors, drenched, smelling of petrichor, her misted half lip moving.

"You know, Guddi, the dead are eternally thirsty, and this rain feels magical." She spoke with a breathy, babyish inflection. "Last month your Papa and I were on a train, and when we saw a bridge, we jumped but got caught in between the trees, the river below us rushing and gushing like a mirage."

"It was a struggle to come out of that tree," Papa complained. He picked up a kitchen rag to dry his slightly wrung neck, his swollen chin.

"Why were you on a train?"

"I don't remember," she said.

•

One morning, in the bathroom, Ma was trying to remove the lipstick stain from her front tooth. Mean strokes and curses. "Where is the bleach?" she inquired.

"Under the sink."

I heard a clink, followed by *good riddance* in Ma's voice. She carried the tooth outside the bathroom and dropped it in the trash box in the kitchen.

"Please draw the curtains, Guddi. You know I can't see when it's so bright."

She covered her eye with the edge of her shirt. Crows fluttered around in the yard, shrieking like djinns, early morning rain blazing on their feathers like oil.

"It's a perfect day. I want the light to come in," I argued.

"As you wish," she said and climbed the stairs. She almost fell and instantly got up, as if a disease was chasing her to a side bedroom where the sun's sting could not reach at this hour.

At night my parents stepped out in the backyard. They traced the hollow in the mango tree where they kept the house keys or used candles and incense sticks, old clips, and a pocket Gita. The trunk was etched with their initials. Running their fingers on the contours, they laughed and kissed like a window had opened in their hearts. The smoke through their rib cages was intense, dark like a rain cloud.

I picked up my purse.

"Where are you going, Guddi?" Ma asked as she entered from the patio door.

"To meet someone," I said.

"Who?"

"It's dark outside." My father teetered, walking up to me.

•

I met Rohan for the first time in a café not far from my home. We'd been talking on social media for weeks. Something came up about families, and I abruptly brought up my parents.

"Yes, you said they live with you."

"They do, except they died six months ago," I whispered, and then looked away to avoid any awkward stare from him.

He cleared his throat. We sat in silence for a few minutes.

"I know someone in our family who travels with his dead wife everywhere," he said and sipped his coffee.

"It's a strange thing," I replied. My cheeks flushed, my heartbeat loud in my chest as if I was confessing to a crime.

"My relative claims you get used to it," he said. "Now we've accepted it too. We serve him with double entrées and appetizers, gifts for both of them." He chuckled like it was a common, amusing thing.

"Though the food stays as uneaten, he insists she tasted everything." Rohan cleared his throat again, as if talking of the dead caught words.

"Perhaps they'll be released if I'm able to disperse their ashes."

"Why don't you?"

"Ma has hidden the urns."

"They don't want to leave you."

It felt like a psychic moment between us, with permission to divulge more. Rohan drank his coffee calmly. His patient, round eyes behind his black-rimmed glasses made me briefly wonder if he saw other worlds too. Outside, the sun had bent down on the road, in shopping malls, on the cars to read faces.

"Ma gets worried when out in the light," I said. "She claims it dismantles her thoughts. So she ends up cleaning daily, her vigilant search for the dirt, impure, the green gloves on her skeletal fingers, her rag picking up dust and scattering it on the floor. Then she gets sick as a dog, squatting over the toilet, puking, shitting, shivering."

"And your father?" Rohan asked, looking interested.

"Papa is friendlier and lazy, following Ma and telling her jokes," I continued. "He goes on all fours to cheer her up and she laughs and laughs, the sound bouncing off her bones and air, absorbed by the walls. At night, they stroll outside, or rather float—I hardly see their legs. Then they come in and play records on an old player. Papa acts like a hero from a black and white Bollywood movie, Waqt, syncing his lips to the lyrics—Aye Meri Zohra Jabeen, the needle dipping on the vinyl like the notes of music touching their delicate frames."

Rohan placed his hand on mine as if he understood.

"Some days Ma is angry because she wants to go out and feel the sun. She gets worked up when near a stove or a fireplace because it reminds her of the crematorium. The relatives and friends kept looking at her, their hands on their mouths, as if keeping their souls in. She kept screaming but no one listened."

I leaned into the chair, breathless, feeling the sweet influx of air. Rohan tipped his head back and sucked on his lower lip as if it were a teat.

•

When I entered the house, it was quiet. I turned on the flashlight to locate the switch. The living room and kitchen were empty. In my parents' room, Ma was weeping. "We thought you ran away," she sobbed, her half face frightened, helpless.

"It was just a date."

"Is he a nice boy?"

I sat for a while with my parents. Ma brought coconut hair oil to the bedroom.

"Do you want to marry this boy, Guddi?" Papa eased into his aaram kursi by the window, raising his wiry arm, donning the side of his face with his mustache. You could see from his sad, reckless gaze that he never grew up with affection from his mother. And Ma never gave him much.

"What's marriage good for anyway?" breathed Ma near my neck as she massaged her skeletal fingers slowly into my scalp. They were small and sharp like the fangs of a vampire I'd seen in movies. "You still hunger for something else, someone else," she said and sighed.

"But you keep your eyes only on each other," Papa asserted.

"The only solace is that you starve together." Ma's fingers combed out a few strands of my hair, smeared them with oil. "There's something intimate about that."

"Even death couldn't part you," I said. My eyes closed; my head was euphoric with the massage. "Now that's love."

Ma laughed. "Guddi, the only true love in this life is for your child. Biological. Anything or everything pales in comparison." She pressed my head with her small fist and hummed a lullaby I used to love as a kid.

It was about one in the morning, and outside the window the moon was milking the clouds. My back was hurting after sitting for a few hours in the same position on the floor. Papa began dozing, Ma's hands were circling slower, her head jerking in and out of sleep. Noisome siesta filled the room. Driven by discomfort, I moved out onto the stairs, grasping my phone, shining its flashlight. In my bed, rushed by thankfulness, I almost gave up the idea of finding their ashes and dispersing them.

•

A few weeks later, I invited Rohan to meet Ma and Papa. Inside the kitchen, he mistook Ma for a barstool on which he put his raincoat. Then, realizing his mistake, he apologized. In response, Ma's leftover muscles twitched. The thin membranes glowed red like a new bruise.

"Ouch, can we have more light in here, please?" Rohan stumbled, hitting his big toe on the dinner table leg.

"The light ruins by revealing everything." Ma started a philosophical discourse. "The dark is discreet, merciful. It lets you be."

"Or indifferent," Rohan said, his pupils expanded, his mouth open staring at the outline of Papa's bones splintered through his flesh, his rotting head. Then he closed his eyes as if swallowing all the violence in their bodies. "I feel hot," he said. I turned the table fan on.

"I'd like to believe the dark is forgiving, all encompassing." Ma walked back and forth like rewound footage. Papa drooled; his saliva collected at the edge of his lip like a slobbering dog.

"I should get going," Rohan said and got up. I followed him outside, almost saying sorry for Ma and Papa's cold attitude toward him, but he stepped ahead of me, signaling to an auto rickshaw at the corner of the street. As the rickshaw revved, he waved at me with a look in his eyes of diminishing hope for something true between us.

When I got back, Papa was on top of Ma on the kitchen floor, her spidery limbs around him, their sounds whispery, weird. The kitchen pulsed with a smell of roadkill, sweat and sex, a morgue with no air-flow. After being around my dead parents for a while, I'd started to recognize each of these smells, but I still gasped, awestruck with disgust.

In my room, I crawled into my bed and texted Rohan.

"Have you reached home?"

He replied after an hour. "You need to let them go."

"Is it because of how they look and smell?"

"Because of how they've dragged you to a gloomy, dark cave and you have every intention of jumping in."

•

"Did you hear back from Rohan?" Ma asked one morning.

"No," I said, and realized she was wearing the nose ring I thought I lost a month ago.

"He is no good, then," she said and caught me looking at her face. "Looks nice on me."

"Please put it back, Ma."

The next day I found the nose ring swimming in my toilet bowl, the crystal like an eye judgmentally and critically staring at me. It looked just like Ma's eyes when she used to hide the jewelry I'd get as a gift on my birthday. She said she was worried I might misplace it, but I knew she was jealous that I looked better wearing the choker or the dangling earrings than she would.

I glanced at the floating nose ring. Then I flushed it away.

•

A squirrel had been digging around the yard. The exposed rim of the copper urn reflected a light in my eyes. I was picking up the mango tree's broken branches from a rainstorm two weeks ago. When I dug them up and looked inside the first urn, I saw my father beneath his skin, way back, back into his childhood, desperate to grow a mustache, the movement in his feet even as he slept, then through a hole in his back, from where I could witness his life as it happened to him, all stuffed into his chest and his heart stretched so thin it was nearly transparent. In the other urn, I witnessed my mother's body, bits of her nails and hair, growing and falling, her mouth's hollow when she had her first orgasm, the little openings in her womb through which the blood oozed when she delivered me, the hope and the frantic in her muscles of being a wife and a mother, the illusions of being happy. I brought the urns inside the house, stacked one over the other, and placed them on the floor in my room. Then I knelt down in front of them while my parents, upstairs, drifted in their dark room like negatives of photos they once were, ribbons of their voices reaching me. Ma shrieked like she was burned alive. Papa groaned like he was beaten, shot, a whistle dying down and rising again. More than their sounds, I heard their misery of neither being dead nor alive, my dread stuck in the same place as theirs. Outside, the monsoon had faded and the sun continued to drink water from lakes, rivers, dried up our wet soil in the backyard. I longed to feel its crackling fire in me.

•

That morning, I locked the house from outside. After Rohan and I emptied the urns in a nearby unnamed creek, the ashes whirled in the wind. My parents' faces flashed in front of my eyes, their skin luminous, beautiful before they disappeared. I sat on the riverbank telling Rohan of my last joyous memory with them: Ma lathering my hair with her favorite Lakme shampoo while Papa ran water in a blue plastic bucket, touching it to make sure it was warm. Ma continuing to slowly rub my head, foam collecting on the bathroom floor like snow, rainbows in the bubbles. It was the only time, besides the oiling of my hair, that I felt their touch for so long, so astonishingly loving. Papa ducking my head under the tap, laughing, and when I came up, catching my breath, Ma pushing me down, playfully trying to drown me. And I knew we were happy, the best we'd ever been.

Rohan dropped me back home, promising he'd come back in the evening to check in. "It's going to be okay," he said before he left.

The house still smelled morbid, so I pulled the curtains and opened the windows. Light rushed in and filled the space like a prisoner set free. Realizing my parents were really gone, I sank to my knees and wept until my voice was hoarse, then a series of hiccups, until I no longer could speak. When I looked up, I saw their silhouettes—bright and luminous, as I saw them in my last vision, a satisfied expression smeared across them, meandering back to their room. Papa's arm was around Ma, and hers was around him, the soft and harmless monsters they'd always been.

"Isn't this what you wanted, Guddi?" Ma said, turning around.

"We couldn't leave you behind," Papa said, twisting his neck.

Something inside me told me I should look away, that they might be just voices in my head, but how could I? Hypnotized, I kept watching them because their eyes were miraculous balls of liquid fire—blue and orange, golden and a hue I couldn't name—every inch of their broken frames rippling with strength, like they belonged to a whole other existence, without suffering. I saw them, then myself in them, inseparable, and a thirst rose in my chest, unquenchable.

CAUTION, PLEASURE CENTER

I LIE NAKED ON the examination table, paper gown crunching against the vinyl every time I move. Goosebumps. I wish I could turn the air conditioning off. I consider getting my phone from my purse lying on a counter next to the tissue box, but the gynecologist might be here any minute. Time is a funny thing. It is written on my thirty-two-year-old skin, each stretchmark a decade, but also there is this: seven years of sharing a bathroom and a closet with Arin, my partner, who at this moment is working from home, his dark-rimmed glasses stuck at the bridge of his pointed nose. His kind, black eyes. Too kind. The last time I had sex with him, he apologized after he came.

Someone softly knocks at the door. The doctor peeps in and says, "I'm sorry, a few more minutes." I nod. On the wall before me is a diagram of female anatomy color coded in shades of pink and yellow, a few strokes of saffron declaring a warning, as if saying, *Caution, pleasure center.*

I move one hand below my navel and place the other on my left breast. *I should tell Arin about Greg. I should tell him I slept with Greg. Each time it was more than the sum of a few and far between sweet fucks.* I sigh, realizing my hands are pressing into my flesh: my heart drums and my thighs pulse, engaged in a duel. The starting and stopping of air conditioning goes on in the background as if unable to decide what to continue.

"Nice to see you," the doctor says as she enters the room. She extends the exam table. I smile and lie down, my feet in the stirrups. A nurse joins us. The doctor sits on a stool, prepared to begin an examination. Discomfort circulates.

"Let's see what's going on in here." She raises her head.

"Yes." I close my eyes, the cold gel smeared into my pink insides. *Greg looks starved and glamourous. Tattoos and piercings. Nothing like my life.* Also true: *Arin has a receding hairline, deepening dimples. Arin cares. Arin is comfort.*

"We'll figure out why you are late," the doctor says, and asks the nurse to draw blood.

I glance as the needle goes in, the tubes fill with rich red fluid. I wonder if it carries all my secrets, if it's double-helixed with my guilt and desire. *You receive what you put out there. It's basic karma. Greg, his lips on my neck, his mouth circling on my breasts, inhaling deeply, his movement on top of me: shadow of a monument coming in and going out of sight. Filling me up with soft, bright explosions. Arin smiling gently at me, his eyes clear, unable to smell my deception.*

The doctor helps me sit up. "You'll hear from us within a week. Anything else?"

"No," I say, my voice suddenly loud. I am still thinking about Greg. The voices from the hallway are amplified: the approaching and receding steps, the shuffling of papers, the opening and closing of doors, secrets spilled in test tubes, plastic cups full of pee pushed in from one side, picked up by a gloved hand on the other, followed by a flush.

Outside, the clouds are dark, ready to burst. I want to hold Arin, but where will that take me? A few years until another Greg walks into my life and I want to stick some part of his body into me. I recall the evening a week ago when I stopped at a pharmacy but never went in to pick up a home pregnancy test. I sat on the sidewalk and waved at a toddler holding his mother's hand walking out of the store. He kept turning and looking at me, waving his tiny fingers. I pulled my knees up to my chest and squinted against the sun until it was mild. On the road, a construction worker periodically turning the board of SLOW and STOP. I pretended it wasn't happening to me, or perhaps I was avoiding finding out until I knew who I wanted to be with or without.

The drizzle taps on my scalp. Next to the parking lot, wet tulips hang their heads, the roads littered with leaves. Inside the car, I try to imagine an impression of a crescent blooming in me: its limbs fused, flesh free of impurities, smooth. The flicker of a heartbeat, cells accumulating on top of each other, a heartbreaking beauty reminding me of my soft insides capable to grow a life, bear its weight and the consequences to come. It's just the two of us here now. The occasional drops flatten on the windshield, breaking apart into a stream of their own.

The lightning comes fast, a thunderclap booms in distance. A sound with a rough edge to it, changing the color and shape of grass, the trees, the cars around me. The rain comes down hard, thick as soup.

I wait for the storm to die, then roll the windows down, inhale the rich scent of freshly soaked earth. The air is thick with sounds of insects, cars on a nearby highway; I notice the limp in the telephone wires, strange possibilities hovering in the voices of the future. I breathe deep, start my car, and turn on the radio. The skyline shifts from a gray outline to countless pinpricks of light, a banana moon hung on the horizon. I scrunch my wet hair, feel hungry at the sight of the water from the road feeding the storm drain like a mouth.

RUINED A LITTLE WHEN WE ARE BORN

OUR MOTHER DELIVERS A boy in the monsoon, we're saved from our father's anger. Our hands are raw, unrecognizable carrying hot water, tugging clean sheets beneath our mother's heels, taut like our names, the smell of her blood and sweaty folds heightened in the air. The baby looks whittled out of a log, his cry a strange-boned hope.

"Why is he crying?" one of us asks.

"We're ruined a little when we're born," the midwife says.

We look at our mother's satisfied face, and the burning in our chests is stronger. If she hadn't delivered a boy, all she'd have is us. Now her mouth pants with a smile, a betrayal.

Outside, our father leans against the banyan, his eyes blinking with insomnia. Ahead, a snake charmer tries to calm a freshly captured female cobra, her hiss a terrible omen had our mother delivered a girl. Eventually, the snake charmer will sedate the cobra before removing her fangs, a small kindness toward the animal.

A Ganesh pooja is organized in our home for the newborn. A black teeka on his forehead to ward off the evil eye of visitors. Our brother looks so peaceful in his sleep, the room bends around him, and we forgive him for a moment. On the patio, there is a stall with sweets and samosas, a cup of chai for everyone except us so there's no shortage of food for the guests.

At night, we hear the trains move in the distance. Coming down the hillside like a long, dark tongue, slamming the levee. One day, we'll slip inside it and travel to a place where we're offered a sky. Our father snores and the baby roots for our mother's breast, his eyes smothered by her flesh. Jealous, we sneak outside and starfish our fingers in the rain-slick earth. Dirt crumbles on our limbs and lips. We tuck it at the edge of our jaws, where our fangs are, pretending we cannot hurt anyone.

Come morning, our mother will drag us to the handpump, overcome by her urge to clean us while the baby cries, smacks his tongue against his lips, hungry. As she drains water from the earth into the buckets, our full-bodied shadows like her stretch marks will cling to her, turning the world full of birds screaming in our throats when she rubs our skin with soap and anger, red and frothy, until she tires out, forgetting the starving baby. We'll run around her in circles, do crazy movements with our hands and legs that'll make her laugh so hard like she used to before our brother arrived. Softly, we'll sink our teeth into her pink flesh until the whites of her eyes turn red and her mouth becomes a loud blur full of wet love only for us.

CALLA LILIES

THE GIRLS SPEAK OF pantyhose and glitter, the girls go on about lace and liquor, the girls run, they fall, rip their stockings, the girls get up, hay in their hair, specks of dirt on their cheeks, breathing the dirty, humid air of the east side of the city, the girls go on about their bruises, on their arms, on their thighs, some above their hearts, the girls knot their hands, the girls shake their booties to "Single Ladies" by Beyoncé, the girls stroke their hair when asked if they are sleeping with each other's boyfriends, *Seriously?* the girls say, rolling their eyes, *you're imagining things, just relax*, the girls slow-mouth, bird breathe, lean in, the girls ring like dull songs in the school hallways, the girls dress up in slinky skirts, pussyfoot and skip class to visit the west end of town where the houses are honey pink with interiors like Pottery Barn, the girls bump against men in dimly lit bars, the girls smoke their cigars, the girls fuck them leaning against the wall or in their trucks shaking loose like the ground after the rain, and later, much, much later, the girls take a drag from the same cigarette, grasp, clutch each other's fingers, *No I'm fine*, the girls say, and crash curses as they flick ash, the girls a swarm of fireflies, pop their light fuses one by one until the cigarette is about done, a red, vanishing tail in the dirt, the girls turn off their sex, blowing white puffs in the small hours of the night until motor bikers with dirty hair and burning eyes stop by and the girls loosen their curls, the girls hope the men will buy them milkshakes and fries because the girls have been drinking beer and now their bodies are lit up with a hot-pink hunger, the girls prance around the leathery chests, the girls rope in the dust from the revving engines, the girls bloom and blossom like calla lilies in a GIF, flapping their arms in the air, their way of saying, saying, *Look at me, look at me!*

A CHORUS OF FLICKERING MOTHERS

IN THE BEGINNING, Nina's mother flickered occasionally. A part of her body, i.e., the edges of her fingers or toes, or her cheek or the curve of her shoulder would start fading—a force, as she'd describe later, pulling the layers of her skin, the nerves below them, and a saw grinding the jail bars of her tendons and bones, then all of it back, then gone again—a switch turned on and off at an irregular frequency. After a few hours, the vibrations would stop altogether, the flesh ruddy, limp. It'd take her weeks to regain the blood circulating in those lifeless parts and yet they wouldn't be fully functional. Nina's father was happy when a corner of her mother's lower lip flickered and vanished. He didn't like his wife's nonstop talking. Finally, he moved around the house with no earbuds.

Nina's mother's mother came to stay with them. She played cards, threw darts, and took walks with Nina. They got Nina's mother tested—blood, spit, stool, a sample of her previously flickered part. Nothing conclusive. Some days, Nina would cry constantly saying she'd lose her mother—not that she got along with her mother or would miss her if she passed on, but the fact that everyone in her school would call her a waif, and her father would marry her off to someone she'd never be able to love. In the following months, Nina's mother struggled to walk with faded calves and blinking toes. Her dangling body parts knocked things over. She tripped after a few steps and wasn't able to get up on her own. Nina's father moved to another town. There was a rumor that he started living with a new woman.

•

Nina's grandma kept the drawers slightly open because she had no fingertips. Years ago, when she was in prison and was denied food as a part of a torture tactic, she sucked on her fingers and bit into them until they bled, tiny bits of flesh keeping her hunger satiated.

When Nina asked her why she was in prison, she laugh-gasped as if stung by a bittersweet memory. "I was in love with another man besides my husband," she said. Despite being in her sixties, Nina's grandma had maintained a mischievous eye movement and youthful prettiness in her personality. She wore her pitch-black hair in a bun, draped in a white sari with creased pleats, with a starched long-sleeved black blouse. Her cheeks glowed with a rose-pink hue, as if she'd applied rouge.

"That was a crime enough," she continued, lifting a handful of wheat flour out of the pantry into a kneading bowl. As the mixer ran, Nina watched the dough, heavy, rising, the pockets of air in between like missing parts of her mother's body and her grandma's fingertips. Outside, the wind and rain rolled the prayer flags on themselves, sunk the lawn like a drenched coat without a warm body.

•

"It's because of prolonged motherhood," Nina's grandma said while trimming the bushes in the garden. "The flickering," she paused, glancing at a long stray branch, "starts in a mother's body after a baby is conceived but is only fatal if her children are demanding."

Nina said she knew she'd been sick with a deadly flu after she turned one. Her mother sat by her pillow day and night, trying to calm her fever down, praying to gods and goddesses, offering her life in exchange for Nina's well-being.

"That's what a mother's supposed to do," Grandma replied and hacked away stray offshoots with her garden scissors haphazardly, "but it has consequences."

"You're a mother too," Nina argued.

"I was away from your mother for many years." Her grandma's voice turned rough, like wind scraping against a tin roof, her neon-yellow gloved hands inspecting the manicured plants and shrubs, her gaze slowly bleeding into something softer as she remembered her husband struck by stroke and then death. His friends claimed he did everything he could to raise their daughter. For a few minutes, the only sounds were the rattling of the scissor hands over each other, missing the branches and cutting the heavy air.

Nina raked away twigs and leaves, and something that looked like a nest, two small eggs, rolled into the street before Nina could catch it. Shells and yolks on the road after a group of cyclists rode away. For a week, there was a squabble of birds outside Nina's window. She often dreamt of a bird flying past the glass, her beak opened like two long blades, searching for her eggs.

•

The rain continued for months. The news channels claimed cracking glaciers in the Himalayan region and reported landslides, washed homes and abandoned cities, skeletons of buildings dangling in floods. "The earth's flickering too," Nina's mother said in a broken, swallowed language, her half upper lip lowered, a train of saliva to her shoulder, her words disappearing like tumbling down from the edge of a tall cliff.

Nina started sleeping with her mother in her father's spot. The mattress had sunk on that side of the bed to an extent that she often rolled off at night. Once she dreamt about her mother turning into a moth, large brown wings with little holes in them. She tried to soar but drifted down and got stuck in between the long, dried roots of a tree that was upside down. When Nina woke, moths were lined up outside the window, some on top of each other, shivering, tangled like necklaces. The yard was covered in a dense fog.

"It's a good omen," Nina's grandma said after listening to her dream. "A tree upside down is a metaphor of taking birth, headfirst. Perhaps the trimming helped with the energy flowing back to the house, rather than from it."

•

Nina's father came back with a pregnant woman. She had the biggest earlobes Nina had ever seen, touching her jawline. It seemed she could pick up the slightest noise, the faintest whisper. She took the upstairs bedroom with Nina's father. Every morning he helped her come down, her long dress sweeping the stairs like a glorious fountain. Together they smiled and licked love from each other's mouths. Nina's mother shrugged it off from whatever was left of her body. "Show-off," Nina's grandma hissed. Her bile surged every time Nina's father cooked a large meal and left the dirty dishes in the sink.

Once Nina's father took the wedding sari from his wife's closet and gave it to the pregnant woman. Nina's mother cried so loud her limp flesh started falling and drifting away in her tears and wails, like pieces of land in a hurricane. Eventually, what was left of Nina's mother was only a pair of eyes crawling on the ground or the walls, sometimes stuck on a ceiling fan until it rotated so fast they hung at the edge of the blade like medallions. Sometimes they glued on the surface of the TV in the living room like permanent damaged spots on the screen against the footage of the floods with dead animals floating in them.

Once the eyeballs drifted outside and slipped into a storm drain. After that day, the rain stopped, and the sun streamed in. But having lost her daughter completely, Nina's grandma groaned, grabbed her anger, and went to Nina's father's room. The pregnant lady was sprawled naked across the bed, her belly, a moon of flesh, soaked in sweat and contractions. Nina's grandma swallowed her grief and helped the lady sit up, stacked pillows behind her curved back. Then she mumbled. Having heard it, the pregnant lady's mouth twitched in horror, her shoulders heaved in fear as her body shivered into quick labor and delivered a son. Nina's father beamed with joy. He held the baby throughout the day, changed his nappies, and brought him to his mother only to feed. He let the lady rest and recover through the humid nights into the wiped-clean dawns, until one afternoon, when the lady was strong enough to walk, she gathered her dresses and told Nina's father that she was in love with someone else. Then she hugged Nina's grandma and thanked her before she left.

"What did you say to her?" Nina's father roared, shuffling his feet uncomfortably, his eyes pythons, shiny balls of war.

"That mothers end up being a pair of eyes trying to follow you everywhere."

In the background, the newborn screamed for his mother's nipples and for a change of clothes. "Shut up," Nina's father shouted, and the newborn screamed louder until the whole house shuddered and settled back as if after an earthquake. Nina's father dropped on his knees like a drooping stick, hugging his head between his arms, unsure what to do next. Then he got up and went outside.

The newborn cried again. Nina's grandma tried to stop Nina, but she rushed to pick up the baby. Cradled in her arm that quivered momentarily, the boy sought her fingers, his touch holier than anything Nina had ever experienced. When she walked out of the room with him, she gleamed mother-like—soft and somehow sinister in her maternal isolation from the world.

"Do you think he'll ever be demanding, Grandma?" Nina asked, her affection for the baby unleashed around her neck like riptides, their pull stronger than the knowledge of her flickering mother reduced to rolling marbles on the floor. "Look," she said to the baby and raised his hand toward her grandma. He smiled, saliva bubbling between his lips.

"Oh, dear," Nina's grandma whispered, warmth up her spine—like pain from an old wound unstitching, strand by strand, staining the edges red.

MAUI

WHEN YOU POSITION YOUR binoculars, feel your toes digging into the sand at Wailea Beach in Maui. When you spot silhouettes in the distance, a mother whale and her baby. When you turn and catch sight of a man on a raft. When you wave. When you go back to the whales and return to the man on the raft, but he isn't there. When you frantically adjust the focus distance and all you see is a blur of ocean. When you consider telling hotel security about the man's disappearance. When your vision has a small blur in the center. When you play the events in your head again and are no longer sure what you saw. When you take the elevator, miss your floor. When you keep alternating between *Fuck* and *I'm sorry*. When the blur seeps into your sleep, and you wake up in the slow torture of the night and look outside your window: the silver-glinted waves as they wash and claim all they can, the TV still flashing on mute. When you stare at the light shifting, darkening under the door of your room. When you check the local newspaper the next day at the breakfast table. When you go back to the beach, sweep the space from frolicking whales to the bodiless ocean emptying into the sky. When you notice the blur merging with other blurs, spreading like a disease. When you keep mouthing *Fuck*. When your eyes feel heavy, your face lit purple in the fading light. When you constantly dream about the man, his overturned raft, his flailing arms in water, his receding voice sucked into the blur. When your nightmares spill and sweat soaks your shirt and you wake sour to his cries. When you feel thirsty and drink the entire twenty-four-ounce water bottle in a long sip. When you are unable to burp, the blur extending from your throat to where the water sits inside you, the gaps in your body you never knew existed. When you smile at your reflection wearily. When you google tragedies caused by tsunamis and hurricanes and you see the buildings submerged in water, the swollen, blue bodies washing up to the shore, faces down, seaweed tangled in the hair. When you realize there's something inexplicably haunting about death by drowning. When the blur has extended everywhere you look. When you watch porn and feel you don't have the energy to stroke your cock. When you find out via WhatsApp that a Bollywood actress was found dead in her half-filled bathtub. When you conclude no amount of water is safe. When the blur is a large whirlpool, drawing your thoughts. When you wonder if the man on the raft wasn't real. When you wiggle your toes, feel the ground. When you see an email from a resort in Maui, offering a three-day package with submarine tours and whale watching. When the blur is a combination of the images of whales clicking, whistling, the ocean seizing and flinging the light back in flaming wet pools like souls of the drowned from hundreds of miles away. When you admit all that calling makes you feel less anxious. When the blur settles high above you like the gray wool of the sky. When you return to the beach, rent a raft, row it further into the ocean, your face spotted by salt, your throat going dry. When you feel no amount of water will be enough. When the blur scrapes the approaching darkness swirling the water black. When you realize how little you know about yourself. When you glance at the shore and wave. When the smudge of people at the beach looks like they are all watching, they are all waving back.

SKIN, BREACHED

THE MAN ARRIVED AT the sewing shop as I was about to close for the day. Ma was inside taking inventory.

"What do you need?" I asked him with an edge of irritation in my voice. After helping my mother with three prom dresses—one the color of the Earth's core, another like the Arabian Sea on a winter morning, the last like a glacier giving the feel of crawling so subtly only the person wearing it would know—I wanted the day to be over.

The man said he wanted a special blanket for his newborn daughter. A cloth as pale and soft as his wife's skin, smelling of her breasts. He brought his wife's picture and her hospital gown to replicate the feel in the fabric.

"Where's your wife now?" Ma stepped out from behind the curtains of a changing room, pulling the measuring tape from her neck, her glasses sliding on her small nose. She lifted the picture of the woman, studying her features. She sniffed the gown.

"She died this evening," the man answered, wiping his tears with an embroidered handkerchief, a border of blue and pink flowers, anagrammed with AJ in the corner, probably his initials.

"I'm sorry," Ma said and opened her notebook. She scribbled about the hues and tints in the woman's skin color, moving the photograph under the lightbulb. She put on her red-colored glasses, fol-

lowed by green and violet to study the lowest and the highest frequency in the picture. "This will take a week," she concluded.

"I don't have much time," the man pleaded. "Maybe until tomorrow. My wife was able to feed my daughter twice before she died, and
since then my daughter refuses milk either from a bottle or a wet nurse.
She cries and cries. I don't wish to lose her." He started sobbing.

"What makes you think this blanket will save her?" Ma placed
her hand on his.

"Perhaps if my daughter smells her mother—" He sniffled.
"Please."

Ma straightened and signaled me to get eyecups. "Here," she
said, "let your tears drop here. Your daughter is as much yours as she
is your wife's. And listen, take me to the morgue. I want to get a sample of your wife's skin, perhaps her eyes too, her nails. I want to smell
her womb and draw some blood," Ma went on, her face lit up, her
voice enthralled with something strange and challenging to work on.

"Whatever you need. I have my car here."

"Leena, close the shop," Ma instructed and tightened her belt
across her tunic. "Wait for me upstairs—we must work through the
night." She smiled at the man with pity and hurried down the steps
into the street. He opened and held the passenger-side door for her,
and in that light Ma looked like a young girl, smoothing the back of
her dress. She got in the car. My hand went up to wave, but she didn't
turn to wave back.

•

It was midnight when someone climbed the front steps. Sleep and
yawns tugged at me. Ma had the keys. It'd been a grueling summer
with too much light so every color looked stonewashed, and with
the start of monsoon, the orders had not slowed down. My mother
charged a handsome amount, but it didn't stop the townsfolk coming

in with never-heard-of designs.

An older man in a uniform followed Ma with a garment bag, a freezer box. After he left, she turned off the fan. "We're going to work with a lot of delicate stuff, so we can't afford the slightest whiff of air pulling things in the wrong direction," she said, and pulled the curtains on the mirrors because she believed if we glanced at our reflections during the construction of objects, they could possess us and erect a barrier to our progress. She lifted the veils when the last stitch was in place.

I laid out the white muslin. "Be careful," she whispered. "This sheer cloth can rip at the slightest tug or nick from a fingernail, Leena."

"Open the window?" I was beginning to feel hot.

"No," Ma insisted. "But if you want, you can take your clothes off."

We stepped out of our dresses. Ma smelled comfortingly of Dettol and cleaning alcohol, though she said she wasn't in the hospital for long, she had to wait outside in the car for a long time. She stooped near the giant thread box and pulled out a few spools labeled in a shivery cursive—tan, beige, hazelwood, oyster, sandcastle. She straightened and slowly unzipped the garment bag. For a moment it seemed empty until a shimmery layer shivered. It was a luminous, thin thing, tinged pink and lavender, a frail husk.

"Skin," Ma whispered, turning her mouth away from the bag. "We can use it to give the sensation of the mother on one side, but first we need to dye the muslin and the padding beneath it to make it look real."

For the next couple of hours, we studied the color, matching the reflection from the skin in her picture, little pores on it like needle marks that stretched and stitched it on a body. Just before the dawn broke, we left the cloth in the dye bath and went to bed.

•

Ma was staring at the eyeballs in the freezer box, most of the ice melted in the heat.

"I want her to watch us while we work so she can guide us."

"She's dead—"

"I know." Ma slipped her arms around me at the waist and drew me close. "But she's watching over her daughter." Her clammy hands drifted, sticking rounded fingernails into the blanket so the baby could feel them on her skin.

"How will you make the blanket smell like her?"

"Watch this," she said, and took a few drops of the man's tears and scratched some fluid from the woman's eyeballs. Then she took a drop of the woman's blood. A whiff of aged cheese with a hint of rosewater floated in the room. I brought in the woman's gown—her sweat dried in the underarms of the linen, dried blotches of milk where her breasts were. It smelled part wet earth, part a parched sky in June, part a fish peeled, its innards laid open. Working with Ma, I'd learned to categorize the exactness in smells. She told me to go on our terrace where the clouds hung low and fill up a jar of them. I did that whenever people wanted something gray and ambiguous—a color and a smell they couldn't describe while they were grieving. The clouds on a humid day were a perfect match of how they felt, or at least they said so. "But this smells like a clear, dry sky," I protested.

"We don't have time right now, Leena," Ma said, a pencil stuck above her right ear, the tip pointed at me.

In the evening, the man sent a car for us. At the hospital, Ma spread the blanket on the wet nurse's lap, and when the newborn was brought in, she cooed and took to the breast in a heartbeat. She sucked the nurse dry and drooled. The man thanked my mother for her effort and pulled out a wad of cash from his pocket. "I am truly grateful," he said. "If there's anything I can do for you—" He held her hands in his and kissed them. Ma's eyes sparkled like they hadn't in a long time. The man was boyish in his face, clean-shaven and well dressed, something about him that my mother confessed later reminded her of Pa.

•

Thereafter, the man whom I addressed as AJ, even though that wasn't his name, stopped by often with his daughter. Sometimes he got expensive dresses and jewelry for Ma, the fabrics she wanted—silk and chiffon, yards of georgette—and while I played with his two-year-old daughter, draping my old dolls in leftover strips of cloth and ribbons, gluing buttons and clips to their artificial hair, he and Ma disappeared upstairs, transmitting the sound of squeaking bed springs, shifting feet, muffled laughter, and crinkles of fabric. When they came down, Ma's face was like a lantern, blood rushing down her cheeks into her slender neck, filling the hollows with a rosy dusk glow. The little girl started calling her Umma. Every time I heard that, my chest burned like the sun swung down a fist and broke my heart. Before the man and his daughter came into our lives, Ma always discussed everything with me, and now she talked about settling down, taking care of AJ and his daughter, closing the shop.

•

One day I took the diamond earrings he gave to Ma on her birthday and buried them in the backyard. When Ma asked if I'd seen them, I refused to tell her.

"Why don't you like him and his daughter?" Ma hissed and pulled my ear.

"I don't," I yelled, and yanked her hand away from me and ran into the yard. I dug out the earrings and threw them at her, an earthworm climbing my wrist. "You don't love me anymore!" She looked at me like I was a stranger, a mistake of the past. Then she hugged me tight and wept.

"I miss your father, Leena," she said, "and now I have a chance to start over." She paused to wipe her tears from the sleeve of her kaftan. "But he's still in love with his wife. And when he's not thinking of her, he's thinking of his daughter."

"You saved his daughter." I sniffled and released the worm in a nearby drain, cleaned my hands and face with a water hose. When I came to the room, a flurry of raindrops had begun. Ma closed the windows. Inside the closet, my hands shuffled through the hung saris and their blouses, satin and linen, lace, nylon with flower prints, drapes of white chiffon in their slots so the cloth could breathe. I pulled out the garment bag.

"Careful." She cleared her throat and covered the mirrors. "I mended the places it got torn off and got it treated with a polish." And I felt close to my mother again, sharing this secret. That evening, we dreamt of her wedding with AJ, his daughter and I as her brides-maids. When the conversation led to her dress, I suggested the skin.

"We couldn't use it for his daughter, but we could use it now."

"It's so delicate—" Her face sulked.

"Remember the quilt you made for Pa before he left for the war?"

"That was my best design," Ma cheered. "The perfume was one-eighth burnt wood," we both whispered, since I'd heard it so many times, "one-sixteenth grass, one-eighth water lilies—his favorite flowers—and rainwater."

"I spun thread out of nettles, weaved cloth from that thread, sewed the quilt from that cloth," she went on as if reciting a long poem, "day and night, through thunder and sunshine, sitting by the fireplace, by the window, on the porch, under a waxing and a waning moon. My fingers burned, my skin prickled, bumps everywhere on my hands bursting with pain. I squeezed blood through the bruises and spread the ache on the fabric, settled my unflinching gaze like a sheen. Once I went up to a lighthouse and tore a piece of sky, patched it on and sealed it with pashmina sprinkled with dewdrops hardened with chemicals." She paused and drew in her breath. "He was so pleased with it. He wore it like a cape. And I nicknamed him Indra, after the rain god."

I placed my hand in hers, my fingers running over hers, imagining the bumps on her smooth skin. "I don't like when AJ's daughter calls you Umma."

"It doesn't matter what she calls me, sweetheart," she turned toward me, "what you and I have *is* sacred." She pointed at the workbench, the spools of multicolored threads and yarns, snaking ropes and tassels, scattered buttons like a sea of eyes. "Ahh, this wedding dress," she sighed, "must be special, Leena. It should be something that brings us closer to what we want. It should bring *us* closer." Her eyes squinted as if taking aim at something far, far away.

"What are you thinking?"

"It should look like water flowing on a body," she said. Leaning in. "Love feels like that, even after it's gone. You're wet with a sensation, no matter how much you pat yourself dry." She raised her eyebrows. "Do you know what I'm saying?"

"You mean when I forget to wipe in between my toes, between my fingers, and feel damp all day long?" I beamed, feeling good about my analogy.

Ma laughed, the whites of her eyes sparkling. "Yes, something like that. You see, love itself has no remembrance, no desire to understand anything but its own rise. Love is erasure of everything else that's known or expected." She studied my perplexed face. "Ah! You'll understand one day." Then her expression changed, matter of fact, cold. "We have to take a trip to study water." She gripped my hand, her pulse over mine.

•

We visited places with waterfalls and rivers, threw stones in lakes, and let our sight track the ripples, swam in throats of warm springs, and signed-spoke to each other below the sparkling surface, floating in and out of our weight. We sat on the beach and charted the razor-edged waves in the ocean, sequined with light before they crashed on the sand and spread like a disease. Ma gave me her journal to keep notes of the shapes and colors, the cool and the hot frequencies within the transparent hues. I asked her if I was ready, and she said she'd been waiting for this moment. Back at home after weeks, while I was fiddling my fingers with silver and platinum threads, she mumbled something about dipping tan threads in an extra thin layer of molten glass. "But of course, they'll be so fragile they might break," she whispered, and shrugged as if it was a bad idea.

•

Time went on and AJ visited Ma without his daughter, spending time with her upstairs, threading her with hope and expectation and thereafter going silent for weeks as if starting over. Ma waited, aging at the corners. Unwilling to communicate with me, she held her dissatisfaction so tight, I was afraid if I poked, she would spill everywhere. Until one day, after months, AJ came in with a young woman and spoke to Ma in the shop. Standing in the kitchen from where I could see her through the glass-paned doors, her frame slumped as she took notes, staring at the door after they left.

"Leena!"

"Yes?"

She held me in her gaze. "This is a request about a wedding gown." She pushed the notebook in my direction. "Do you recall the one we imagined?" She got up and locked herself in the bathroom.

When she stepped out, I shook her shoulders. "Ma, he can get the dress from somewhere else. Why you?"

"Because I have the skin," she said, so softly I thought I imagined hearing it. I leaned toward her.

"You didn't tell—"

Her eyes went past me, to the window. She lowered her brow. "You'll finish," she said, with a little curt nod, and looked at me with the precision of a missile. "Won't you?"

•

Before, when we worked on specific dresses and weren't sure how the color would turn out, Ma worked on the same dress in the day and at night. "There's this seam between dusk and dawn, a thin edge of barbwire that you have to cross back and forth to get the true colors."

So, I worked on the fabric during the days and rested in the evenings. I woke up in the middle of the night and worked again. After countless trials, I achieved the exact color in the dye bath. One night after Ma was asleep, I sat on a chair beside her bed and watched her body swimming in a slow, rhythmic breath, traced an outline of her skin in the air with my index finger. *This is how the dress should be, only visible to the one with complete focus.* I traced the outline several times until I was certain of the nooks, a body expanded and contracted while breathing. Reminded of the time when Ma and I worked almost naked all night, I took off my clothes and slipped under the covers with her. She turned in her sleep and placed her arm around my waist, and it grew heavy, sticky with sweat, unbearable. In those hours, approaching sleep and waking up intermittently, I dreamt of all the colors and smells rushing to a center. Pieces of me flying from different seasons and terrains, past lives magnetized toward that center. Everything collapsed into me, imploding, the walls like playing cards falling inward in slow motion, forming a ghost seeking a skin.

The crowing of roosters wrecked my ears in the orange haze of dawn. Ma was drinking coffee at the kitchen table. The humidity was supposed to get worse. She didn't comment when, wrapped in a sheet, I checked if all the windows were closed and pulled the curtain and started to work on the dress. Day after night, and another night after that, I poured my light into the dress. I poured the affection from Ma that made my waist numb, the prickly sensation of jealousy and loneliness I'd accumulated when AJ and his daughter came close to Ma. I threw in the sound of *Umma*. I pushed in the anger of constructing Pa in my mind, with my mother's memories like a second-hand detail. I stitched it all on the inside with threads sharpened with crushed glass—microscopic shards, enough to rupture one layer of skin of the bride, then another, and another, snipping the seams that sewed a body with life. Little earthquakes. It would be a matter of hours when the blood would first trickle, weaving warm on the skin like a basket, then in ribbons, eventually gushing everywhere, until the heart was a hole unable to sing.

It was noon, two days later, when I finished—crushed glass on my fingers, on my arms, on my cheeks—dried, red drops. The dress stood inside the garment bag, the zipper open: its outline like tendrils of smoke, but as you got closer, vein-like threads shone behind the skin and reflected the light around them. Light pressed against my eyelids. Light pressed on my skin like squeezing a beetle into glitter with your fingers. I ran out of the room into a cold shower. Water drummed against my spine, stings everywhere.

When I got out, Ma was sitting by a closed window. "There you are," she said, and pulled me close, kissed my forehead, the corners of her mouth turned up, the sinews in her neck tender as butterflies, a live wiring of veins. Her hands descended down my shoulders like something as divine as hope. I wanted to ask her if this was where she held Pa—his loss as her belonging, and if this was where AJ had reached and soured her spine with longing again. Instead, tears streamed down my cheeks, the spaces between my toes wet.

"Look here," she said, and lifted my face. Her skin was a hue of hummingbird red, a layer already growing beneath it waiting for the first to shed. *How many lives did the skin have? How did it know to thread in one direction to grow and fall, and leave the pain behind?*

"I hope the bride likes the dress." She leaned forward, her shiny black eyes at once inquisitive and remote as if this conversation was not from a mother to her daughter but from one seamstress to another.

"Why wouldn't she?" I replied, too quickly. Ma gave me a defiant look, daring me to divulge more. In that moment, an acute competition shuddered into being, a rupture as quiet as eyes blinking or an old skin dissolving into dust. Perhaps she saw, too, that my childhood was over, and the knowledge seeped into my bones, tightening my chest, racing my heart.

"Yes, why wouldn't she?" Ma said, studying me long enough to let the familiarity of the love I had known be sliced by a blade of envy.

"Would you like to try it on?" I felt ashamed of asking such a question. But something inside me kept pushing my words out of my mouth to see how far I'd go to make her believe in my skill. To make her feel proud of me, to assign meaning to myself.

"Now, why would I?" The murky light and stuffed air swelled around us, suffocating me with her authority.

"Because it feels like love, Ma," I said, and opened the window wide.

ACKNOWLEDGMENTS

MY FOREVER GRATITUDE TO the editors of the following publications, in which portions or all of these stories first appeared, sometimes in slightly different versions and titles:

Mother, False | *Post Road*; Girl with a Painted Tongue | *Fictive Dream*; Fever | *Variant Literature*; Ghosts of the Unborn | *EX-POST Magazine*; Shabnam Salamat | *Witness;* Bubblegum | *X-R-A-Y Lit Mag*; One Milky Window | *Forge Literary;* Cow's Tongue | *Copper Nickel*; Tornado, Falling | *Cape Cod Review*; OB-GYNs I Loved | *Jellyfish Review*; Mother, Galaxy X | *New World Writing*; It Rained That Day | *Bluestem*; Milky-eyed Orgasm Swallows Me Whole | *Parentheses*; Punya Mitti | *Shenandoah*; Saanwalee | *Margins AAWW*; My Mother Visits Me in America and Is Annoyed by What the Dishwasher Can Do | *OKAY Donkey*; Lawns, Maui | *No Contact*; 20mph | *Moon City Review*; Storm Warnings | *Cincinnati Review Micro*; Swallow | *Chattahoochee Review*; White Ash | *The Rumpus*; Potholes in the Sky | *Chestnut Review*; Barely Formed | *matchbook*; Sing Me A Happy Song | *Master's Review*; Earth's Tears | *Alien Literary Magazine*; Ground Zero | *Arkansas International*; Stranger and the Green Gloves | *Prime Number*; It's Crucial Where You Hang That Mirror | *Los Angeles Review*; Mother, Lost | *Electric Literature*; Soft, Harmless Monsters | *Southeast Review*; Caution, Pleasure Center | *Brink Literary*; Mother, Prey, Ruined a Little When We Are Born | *CRAFT*; Calla Lilies | *Salt Hill*; A Chorus of Flickering Mothers | *Denver Quarterly*.

Thank you to The Rights Factory and my agent Natalie Kimber and Tamanna Bhasin for their tireless efforts to bring this book into the hands of various publishers in its best form possible.

My deepest appreciation and thanks to Michelle Dotter, editor of DZANC Books, for saying yes to this collection, and for her insightful reading and her eye for perfection. Thanks to Chelsea Gibbons for her several rounds of sharp edits and suggestions.

Thank you to Sarah Shields for creating a breathtaking, perfect cover of this book.

Thank you to the writing community that fosters inspiration and constructive feedback and brings joy to me by reading and sharing every story I have written. Thank you for your loving support.

Infinite love and thanks to my children who have read several initial drafts of these stories and given their critique. Endless gratitude to my husband and my parents.

ABOUT THE AUTHOR

Tara Isabel Zambrano is a South Asian writer and the author of a full-length flash and short story collection *Death, Desire, and Other Destinations* by OKAY Donkey Press in 2020. She lives in Texas and is an electrical engineer by profession.